WHEN HEAVEN
INVADES
HELL

JOSHUA RASMUSSEN

RACHEL RASMUSSEN

Published by Great Legacy Books

Great Legacy Books
www.greatlegacybooks.com

ISBN: 978-1-7323834-0-1

First Edition: May 2020

10 9 8 7 6 5 4 3 2 1

ACKNOWLEDGEMENTS

We are grateful to Amy Duncan, Joey Rasmussen, Marge Rasmussen, Gabriella and Lucas Senra, Jerry Walls, and Craig Weishaar for their inspiration and valuable feedback on an earlier draft of this book.

We are grateful, also, for countless other idea leaders and friends who have helped refine our conversations and thoughts over the years, leading to the development of many of the ideas in this book.

The production of this work would not have been possible without all of you.

CONTENTS

This book is dedicated to the Noble and the Hopeful people of planet Earth.

PREFACE

GIVEN THE PROVOCATIVE TITLE of this book, you may be wondering what to expect as you open the pages that follow.

First, we want you to know that this book is fiction. Our goal is not to try to show that some particular sequence of events is real. Rather, we use a story to expose patterns of two opposing kingdoms: the kingdom of darkness, and the kingdom of light.

Second, this is not an ordinary fiction book. The settings, characters, and events serve as a stage for a drama of ideas. You will discover that the central focus of the story is the exploration of ideas surrounding a central question: *what is the destiny of souls?* In our story, we provide a context for exploring views of the afterlife from new angles. We hope that the ideas presented in this book will inspire new layers of understanding of the greatness of God's purposes for all souls, both present and future.

Third, we are aware that every reader will come to this book with unique perspectives and experiences, along with sets of convictions, speculations, expectations, and concerns surrounding the topic of the afterlife. We have intentionally written this book with many different sets of beliefs in mind. Consider this book as an opportunity to entertain some interesting and provocative ideas with fresh eyes and an open heart.

We now present to you, *When Heaven Invades Hell*. Enjoy!

Sincerely,
Rachel and Joshua Rasmussen

CHAPTER ONE
God's Strange Question

YOU SEE THEM from a distance—a vast multitude. You don't know who they are, or where they are going. They sparkle like stars in a galaxy. Their energy allures you.

As you imagine joining them, you suddenly find yourself walking in their midst. They are people of light, embodying diverse appearances and expressions. In their presence, you feel love, acceptance, and peace. You get the sense they are traveling toward a special place that is beautiful and good.

Out of curiosity, you peer ahead into the distance. A green landscape of rolling hills unfolds before you. A grand city glistens on the horizon.

"That is where they are going," you say to yourself.

Everyone moves leisurely, yet within a moment the people have made their way across the field and are approaching a grand gate of pearl. As the people of light draw near the gate, the gate opens to let them through.

Your heart leaps as you step closer to the gate. Everything inside you longs to see what lies beyond the gate.

As you approach the threshold, a quiet voice from the center of your being arises. "You are not ready," the voice warns gently.

You stop. Those around you continue to move through the gate. Within a moment, the final ones are passing you by and disappearing from your sight.

You strain to see where the people of light are going, but you can no longer distinguish their forms from the glorious light emanating from the city beyond. How can you turn back now? Your desire to enter through the gate is difficult to contain.

Your soul speaks, "Where are they going? I want to go with them."

The inner voice replies, "You do not understand what you ask for. Know this: what lies ahead will be the greatest event in all of history. You are not yet ready to take part in it. However, your curiosity will give you sight."

At the speed of thought, you are reunited with the people of light. You turn around and see the crystal skyline of the city behind you. Under your feet is a street of gold so pure it almost looks transparent.

To your left you see a grand building. Each face of the building has carvings depicting history and purpose. Above the main entrance of the building is written: *The Hall of Records and Decrees.*

One particular carving near the base of the building captures your attention. In the center is a planet. Around the planet are beings with wings, looking toward the planet with expressions of compassion and wonder. On the planet are two trees. Standing between the two trees are two people—a man and a woman.

"Who are they?" your soul asks.

The inner voice answers quietly, "These are the first ones to rule on the planet, Earth."

You press for more. "What is the meaning of the trees and the beings with wings?"

A story unfolds within you. You observe many events in your mind's eye. You are watching highlights of the human story, from its beginning to the present time. The scene is so captivating that you are entranced by it.

You see two paths God's children can take. One path leads to life. The other path leads away from life.

You feel the uncertainty and hope carried by the winged beings watching the events on Earth unfold. But you are left wondering, "Why would God's children be presented such an obvious choice? How could they not choose love? How could they not choose life?"

Sensing the multitude moving farther away from you, you make the conscious decision to set aside your many questions and move on.

You follow the people of light as they enter into a clearing. The ground is now pure and smooth, like marble. Far in the distance, thick, white pillars extend upward and disappear into the sky. The proportions are difficult to grasp.

As you walk toward the distant pillars, white and gray mist accumulates, soon covering the marble floor in a thick blanket. Brilliant rainbows glimmer and dance in the midst of the pillars ahead. A sweet fragrance greets you as you approach.

You wonder in your spirit, "Where am I?"

A quiet voice answers, "You are in the *Outer Courts of the Heavenly Temple.*"

With awe and wonder, you continue forward, through the pillars. Ahead, you see a wide platform, with stairs lining every edge. Surrounding the platform are golden bowls for burning incense. Many creatures of diverse forms are gathered around the platform. The people of light ascend the short flight of stairs and arrange themselves comfortably on the platform, nearly filling it completely. As your feet touch the steps, you gain the awareness that you are now entering the *Inner Courts of the Heavenly Temple.*

With every step, you feel increasing weight resting upon you. Yet, you feel your strength increasing. Without this new strength, you sense you would be crushed. But this weight is not a weight of burden. It is the weight of glory. Your natural response is one of reverence. This is a very special place.

You take your place among the multitude of people in the Inner Courts. "What will happen next? Why are we here?" you wonder. You are grateful that you have been permitted to stand among the glorious beings in this place.

In the quietness, you gain an inner knowing concerning what is about to happen. *Today is the day of new revelation.* This is one of many appointed times for this purpose. During these appointed times, the creatures in the Inner Courts learn about new assignments and purposes. They also learn more about the true nature of everything. The Source of All is about to reveal something new.

Your spirit quickens. Suddenly, a brilliant light appears in the midst of the pillars. Every creature—great and small—looks toward the glowing light emanating from the center of the pillars. You gaze into its brilliance, curious to know what it is. You are surprised its brilliance does not overwhelm you.

As everyone faces the light, a voice from the light begins to speak. As the voice speaks, a gentle energetic current runs through your body from head to toe.

The voice from the light is familiar. This voice is the same guiding voice you have heard inside you for as long as you can remember. This is the voice of the Lord.

What the voice says surprises all who are gathered in the Inner Courts. Instead of revealing a new truth, the Lord asks a question:

"How would you feel if I offered a separated soul a body of life and a place with us?"

The question weaves through the multitude like a trail of sparkling ribbon. The question lingers until each person feels its depth and significance.

You sense the people around you responding with many thoughts and feelings. They are wondering why the Lord proposes a question rather than revealing a new truth, as everyone expects. They are also pondering the question itself. The question is most peculiar. *Could a separated soul be given a body of life?*

Three primary questions emerge from the multitude as they consider the Lord's question:

"Why are we being asked if a separated soul can join us?"

"Is this a test?"

"How could a separated soul be given a body of life?"

Everyone is wrestling with the apparent contradiction of inviting a soul who has chosen the path of darkness to take a place with the people of light.

In addition to the questions, you also sense a mixture of strong beliefs from various individuals. You catch the thought of a person near you. The thought carries a taste, which is somewhat bitter, somewhat sour, and somewhat salty:

> "I feel such an offer would
> violate perfect justice."

As you experience the thought, its flavor fills you. Is this thought also your own thought? You cannot tell whether you alone can taste this thought, or whether others are tasting it as well.

All the people look toward the light in the center of the pillars. Together, they invite the Lord to resolve the tension they feel.

Strangely, the light merely pulsates with brilliant colors, but says nothing.

Pure love fills the atmosphere of the temple. In the midst of uncertainty, you feel the sturdy bonds of trust between all the people and the Lord.

Even still, the multitude remains curious. Today is the day of new revelation. Yet, instead of revelation, there is a question without an answer. In the Inner Courts, there has never been a question without an answer.

The multitude's thoughts and feelings coalesce into the following message directed to the Lord:

"You, oh Lord, are both awesome and wise, far beyond our comprehension. You ask us how we would feel if a separated soul were granted a way into our kingdom. We have many feelings, and they splinter through different perspectives. We are curious to know your thoughts, Lord. What do you see?"

The message travels toward the light. Everyone watches.

The light glows brightly as it envelops the message into itself, but the light remains silent.

The heavenly creatures desire to hear the Lord's response, despite the silence. No one doubts the Lord's goodness, even in this vulnerable moment of uncertainty.

As you look toward the light, you hear a quiet sound. It is like a low rumble. It grows stronger and more distinct. You realize it is coming from the light. The sound is laughter. Joyous laughter. The laughter grows louder and deeper. It is powerful and emotional.

The Lord's laughter is contagious. All the people in the Inner Courts also begin to laugh.

A playful, light-hearted joy wells up within you. You cannot contain the steady stream of laughter emerging from deep in your belly.

You see every being—great and small—laughing. Some exhibit a playful demeanor, while others have a regal appearance. None are immune to this tangible joy.

In the midst of gladness, however, curiosity remains. Every creature is wondering, "What is the meaning of this laughter?"

CHAPTER TWO
Disagreement in Heaven

SOMETHING CATCHES your eye. You look up, and there before you is an image in midair. The image appears amidst the pillars, above the multitude. The image first appears as a bright sun. Then, alongside the sun appears a moon. Finally, the moon begins to eclipse the sun so that only the sun's outer rays shine through.

An angel flies into midair to face the multitude. The angel asks, "Do any of the sons or daughters of Adam know the meaning of this sun, or of the moon covering over it?"

You hear voices calling back in the distance, "Tell us the meaning. We do not know it."

The angel descends toward the bright light of the Lord in the center of the temple courts. As the angel approaches the light, his shape disappears in the glowing brilliance of it. The angel re-emerges from the light, radiating like liquid metal. His wings flap until he is again hovering in midair before the multitude. He announces in a loud voice:

"All who have ears to hear, listen to the message of the Eternal One, the Ever-Living Source, who appears to us as light. The sun is the hope that is firmly rooted in your souls. This hope grows from the seed of love. True love hopes for all things pure, good, excellent, and true. This hope is the brilliant sun shining in the air amidst the pillars of the temple.

"But there is something else firmly rooted in your souls. From the seed of love, righteousness and justice also grow. Righteousness and justice appear as a moon. Just as the moon reflects the sun's glory, so righteousness and justice reflect the glory of your everlasting hope.

"However, there is a great mystery yet to be understood. Righteousness and justice reflect your glorious hope. But do righteousness and justice also block your hope? Do the righteousness and justice that grow from love eclipse the hope that grows from that same love?"

The angel lingers in the air while the multitude ponders the interpretation of the scene.

You hear from some of the people near you, "Forgive us, for we still do not understand the meaning of these things."

With outstretched arms, the angel replies, "May the Lord grant you understanding."

Just then, a ripple of energy gently rolls outward from the light through the Inner Courts.

As the ripple passes through you, you hear poetic words within you:

"Amidst the beauty, there is
pain. Amidst the joy, there is
sorrow."

The light speaks audibly now with a sound that resonates throughout the temple:

"Look, and understand the meaning of the eclipsed sun. This sun is the hope of the multitude. Many of you hope that a separated soul can be restored and given a place with us."

The image of the eclipsed sun rises higher and grows to twice its original size.

The voice continues:

"This sign of the eclipsed sun is from you. Hope is vibrant among you. Yet, a vast number of you wonder whether the demands of righteousness and justice eclipse all hope for the restoration of a lost soul."

From the multitude, a heartfelt cry emerges. "Tell us, Lord. What can we do?"

The light gives no reply.

In the absence of a reply, tension begins to build in the Inner Courts.

"The task of rescuing a separated soul is impossible," some of the people reason.

Others speculate, "Perhaps the grace of God can overpower the constraints of justice."

You realize there is a growing disagreement in the courts of heaven. Tension is increasing.

Yet, in the midst of opposing feelings and ideas, a song arises from the multitude. The song is beautiful, with harmonies you have never before heard. The song expresses emotions of unbreakable love. This love is all the more spectacular in the midst of the disagreement.

The song of unity transforms into a song of worship. Everyone sings:

> *You are perfect in all of your*
> *ways.*
> *No one can see the edges of*
> *your wisdom.*
> *To you be all glory, honor, and*
> *praise, forever.*

The light coming from the center of the temple begins to transform. The Source of All takes the form of a great Lion.

The Lion is large. He towers over the heads and shoulders of everyone in the temple.

As the multitude continues to worship, the Lion paces in the midst of the people.

The Lion's voice adds to the song like a low drum, repeating a pattern built from a single query: *"Which one? Which one? Which one? Which one?"* He speaks in a low voice that shakes the ground.

The song builds in energy. The Lion listens and absorbs the beautiful sounds proceeding from the mouths of the multitude. Anticipation rises as the Lion returns to the center of the temple.

The singing continues. In the midst of the song, you hear a quiet voice say in your heart, "The time has come for a case to be made in the temple courts."

You look back toward the center of the temple. The Lion is nowhere to be seen.

The singing gradually lulls. The people look toward one another, wondering what to do next.

From somewhere within the multitude, a humble voice suggests, "The Lord trusts us to decide how to proceed. Let us choose representatives to speak on our behalf. These representatives will lay out all the considerations of our hearts with skill, wisdom, and love."

"Yes, let us do this," many reply.

Thoughts take on forms and colors around the people. Similar thoughts merge together. People with similar thoughts draw nearer together.

Two primary forms of thought emerge around two groups. One group has the hope that a separated soul can be restored to life. The other group has the assurance that a separated soul can never be restored.

Those who maintain hope of rescuing a separated soul are called by all the rest, "the Hopeful." Those who maintain assurance that no separated soul can be rescued are called by all the rest, "the Noble."

Within each of the two groups, wise ones are chosen. These wise ones discuss who is best qualified to represent the thoughts and feelings of their group. You are amazed by the humility and grace displayed in their interactions.

After a brief time, the two groups choose their representatives. Moses will speak on behalf of the Noble. Adam will speak on behalf of the Hopeful.

Chapter Three

The Noble Speak

YOU FEEL A PROMPTING in your heart: "Invite the Noble to speak."

Your heart agrees. Immediately, you see a glowing energy arc leap from your center, across the length of the temple, toward the epicenter of the Noble crowd. You see a similar energy emerging from others. Everyone's energy travels toward the same location.

The glowing energy surrounds Moses, who has been chosen to represent the Noble. As the energy swirls around him, the people of light cheer in encouragement. Not one remains silent.

The energy and love condenses around Moses, forming a sort of armor. The armor absorbs into him, strengthening him as he walks toward the center of the Inner Courts.

The multitude continues cheering.

As Moses approaches the center of the Inner Courts, a platform rises up from the ground in the center of four pillars. The platform is round, measuring about six meters across, and lined with stairs. The platform rises into the air to the height of half a man, and there it awaits Moses' arrival.

You study the man as he approaches the platform. His skin is burnished bronze, and his hair is a dark, dusty brown. His eyes are large, round, and defined. His nose is broad. A thin black line of close-shaven hair outlines the upper edge of his tan lips. Long locks of hair fall in gentle waves across his forehead, behind his ears, and down his back, and his chin wears a beard that covers his chest. The folds in his dark red robe sway gently as he walks.

Moses firmly plants his feet on each step as he ascends the platform. His stance is confident, yet humble. His face is softened with empathy and compassion. His body carries boldness and strength to defend and advance the purposes of the Lord.

Moses bows his head. After a moment of stillness, he lifts his countenance and addresses the multitude:

> "Citizens of the kingdom, we are in the midst of love and wisdom and power. In this temple, worship ascends to the Lord day and night, and only those who seek the Lord enter into these Inner Courts. We have one spirit and purpose.
>
> "Yet, we face a challenge. The Lord has asked us a question. *Can a separated soul be given a body of life and a place with us?* Our perspectives diverge, and resolution appears to require a contradiction.
>
> "However, in this place, truth reigns. Therefore, let us rejoice, for the Lord has properly prepared us with everything we need!"

Moses' voice is stately, with a deep resonance. His voice carries authority.

His face is shining with brilliance. You see both strength and beauty in him. You are struck by every curve and shadow of this man's face. Every line has meaning. Every feature carries depth and purpose. The countenance of this man alone testifies to ages of experience he has enjoyed and endured with the Lord. You ponder how such a layer of depth is possible by a mere arrangement of shapes. But is it the shapes alone that tell the story of this man? It is hard to tell. All you know is that by simply gazing upon Moses, you have absorbed layers of understanding about the Lord that you have never before known.

Moses speaks again:

> "It has been assigned to me to represent the case of the Noble. I agree to carry this responsibility with care and humility, in service to the citizens of heaven, and in service to the Lord God Almighty. It is an honor to stand before you."

Moses bows to the crowds in a spirit of reverence and service. Moses' love for each person in the temple courts is felt by all.

The multitude sends ripples of love and approval toward Moses like waves on an ocean. An invitation arises from the multitude as a thought form: "Moses, tell us what you see."

Moses nods. He stretches out his hand. Suddenly, a large staff appears in his hand. He points his staff toward each of the four pillars surrounding the platform where he is standing. He proclaims with boldness:

> "These, my friends, are pillars of divine wisdom upon which the entire creation rests. These pillars contain the knowledge, wisdom, principles, and decrees of the Lord Almighty. From these, every mystery in heaven and on Earth can be unraveled. The wisdom within these temple courts, hidden within its pillars, is continuously being revealed to God's creation. This wisdom has been established before the foundation of the world.
>
> "Each pillar contains infinite wisdom, but no pillar contains all wisdom. Together the pillars will give us the answer to the question before us. It is upon these pillars of wisdom from the Lord that I will rest the case of the Noble."

Moses looks toward the floor of the Inner Courts and points downward with his staff. "Look below you, children of the Most High."

Those around you look down, and you look down as well. Below your feet is a feeling of warmth. Letters spontaneously etch into the glassy stone under your feet. The engraving reads, "LOVE."

Moses straightens his posture, then continues:

> "Listen carefully, royal citizens. The pillars contain the wisdom of the ages. But these pillars do not stand alone. The foundation of these timeless pillars of wisdom is *love*. Without love, there is no wisdom. Love grows wisdom, and wisdom rests on love."

Moses collects himself. "Now, let us consult the first pillar."

Moses directs his staff toward the pillar on his left, slightly behind him. Moses speaks to the pillar: "Open!"

The pillar glows. A glittering mist surrounds the pillar. Then the pillar opens, like a pair of double doors as tall as the sky. A cloud pours out of the pillar, and within, a large scroll is revealed. The scroll is thick and tall, and tightly rolled. No creature has the strength or wisdom to carry the scroll, or to open it, or to exhaust its contents. The scroll is too vast in its dimensions for anyone but the Lord Himself to master the entirety of it.

"Lord, have mercy on your servant," prays Moses, with reverence.

A gentle whisper floats through the atmosphere of the temple for everyone to hear:

> *"The Spirit will guide you into*
> *all truth."*

Just then, the scroll inside the pillar glows brightly. Moses begins to glow with even greater brilliance than before.

Moses turns once again toward the multitude. He breathes in deeply, and then addresses the crowd:

> "Listen, friends. The question the Lord has set before us is a test for the wise. *How would we feel if a separated soul were given a body of life and a place with us?* To answer this question, we must understand the wisdom of love. The wisdom of love gives love order. Where there is love, there is order. Where there is no love, there is no order. Without love, there is only chaos. I will now reveal to you the order in love."

Moses points again to the pillar and announces,

"The name of this pillar is *Justice*."

As Moses looks toward the pillar, the pillar's glow reaches toward him and encapsulates him. Moses opens his mouth, drawing the pillar's glow into himself with his breath. The wisdom of the pillar permeates his being. The energy of the pillar suits him. You can tell that Moses is well-acquainted with this wisdom.

Moses begins a speech:

> "Can a separated soul be rescued? It is not possible. Why is it not possible? Because perfect love contains perfect justice."

Moses' expression is bold, but he continues gently.

> "Without justice, love has no meaning. Justice is the guardrail that separates love from hate. The separated souls hate everything good. They hate wisdom, virtue, and each one of us. They also hate each other. They constantly scheme to harm each other. Their hatred does not mix with love. Souls that hate everything good must be separated from everything they hate, if the conditions of perfect justice are to be met.

"Justice requires separation between good and evil. If good and evil were never separated, then the agents of light and the agents of darkness would never get what they deserve. The righteous would not enjoy the fruits of their righteousness, and the evildoers would not reap the consequences of their evil schemes.

"Separation is part of creation. In the beginning, there was no separation. The Lord spoke, and at His word, there was separation: light separated from darkness, sky separated from sea, and sea separated from land. Separation brings order out of chaos. Without separation, there is chaos.

"Hear me, oh saints. If the dark souls were to join us, darkness would mingle with our thoughts and feelings. Hell would invade heaven.

"Listen carefully: there is no justice when hell invades heaven."

At these words, about two thirds of the citizens of the kingdom, including many standing with Adam, nod in agreement with

Moses' argument. About a third of the multitude remains still.

Moses strokes his beard in contemplation. Feeling the divided opinions of the crowd, he turns to the second pillar. He lifts his staff and points at the pillar on his left, slightly in front of where he stands on the platform. The pillar sparkles and glows.

"Open!" Moses commands. The pillar opens. A large scroll, as grand as the first, is revealed inside. A white cloud pours out from the inside of the pillar onto the temple floor. Moses gazes toward the glowing scroll. The wisdom from the scroll reaches toward Moses, and he welcomes its engulfing embrace.

Filled with renewed strength and joy, Moses turns to face the crowd. He motions toward the second pillar with his staff and says,

"The name of this pillar is *Revelation*."

Moses proceeds to explain how the revelation of the Lord pertains to the redemption of separated souls. This is the case Moses presents:

"Our Lord does not lie. He does not deceive. Now consider the Lord's revelation to the inhabitants of Earth.

"The Lord declared that there would be a day of separation—a time when the light would be distinguished from darkness. This is the day of judgement— the day of the separation of the sheep from the goats. Listen to this account:

"The King says to the sheep, 'Come into your inheritance. For when I was hungry, you gave me something to eat, and when I was thirsty, you gave me something to drink, and when I was a stranger, you invited me in.' But to the goats, the King says, 'Depart from me, you who are cursed, into the eternal fire prepared for the devil and his angels. For when I was hungry, you did not give me anything to eat, and when I was thirsty, you did not give me anything to drink, and when I was a stranger, you did not invite me in.'"

As Moses reads, the words are written in the sky in golden letters. You admire the beauty of the words as they glisten.

You understand the firm nature of the words as they display before you. They are stronger than diamond. No power can destroy the words, or even alter them. The words are sustained by the Lord Himself.

Moses continues:

"By this revelation, we understand that there is a separation. Some enter into the everlasting fire, separated from the presence of the Lord forever. This condition is the state of all those separated souls who now occupy hell. Others enter life, as you have.

"Just as the Lord separated the light from the darkness on the day of creation, so the Lord separates the light from the darkness on the day of judgement.

"The Lord has revealed that all separated souls go to a place where 'the worms that eat them do not die, and the fire is not quenched.' The beloved apostle John has recorded the testimony of the Lord that 'the smoke of their torment rises forever and ever.' And to the prophet Daniel, the Lord revealed that at the time of the end, multitudes would awaken from the dust of the earth, 'some to everlasting life, others to shame and everlasting contempt.' Therefore, if our place in heaven is secure, then likewise is the place of the separated souls in hell secure.

"Understand, my fellow citizens of the light, eternal torment is the only possible outcome for souls who have separated themselves from the love of God. For without love, only torment remains. Only perfect love can cast away torment. But since the separated souls have rejected perfect love, no hope remains. There is no turning back, for as it is written, 'man is appointed once to die, and then to face the judgement.' This judgement is final."

There is a reverent silence among the multitude. Moses continues:

"Hear, everyone, the revelation contained within the history of Earth. Kings and queens of heaven, consider the revelation of the Lord we have encountered. The Lord cannot lie. The Lord cannot deceive. The wisdom of the Lord that fills the earth cannot be a lie."

After a brief pause, Moses lifts his staff toward the pillars on his left. He declares with boldness,

"As you can see, the pillars of Justice and Revelation stand in perfect accord."

Moses' case sits heavy in the room. Despite this, every person in the Inner Courts affirms Moses and encourages him in spirit.

Strengthened, Moses points his staff to the third pillar, which is on Moses' right side, slightly behind him. This pillar glows as Moses commands, "Open!" Inside, there is another scroll likened unto the previous scrolls. A misty white cloud rolls out of the pillar, adding to the misty layer already covering the temple floor.

"Listen, my friends," Moses says as he turns his body to face the multitude squarely. "There is more wisdom to love."

He steps to the side of the platform and gestures toward the newly-opened pillar. Moses points to the pillar and proclaims,

"See this third pillar. The name of this pillar is *Liberty*."

Moses invites the wisdom of this pillar into him, and the wisdom readily sets upon him. Moses is radiating a brilliant light, yet the light is not harsh to look at.

Moses turns again to face the multitude. He introduces the wisdom of the pillar of Liberty.

"We saw that justice separates love from hate. Yet there is another reason for separation."

Moses then points his staff out to the crowds. "The Lord has imparted to one of you the grace to present the wisdom of this pillar of Liberty in a special way that I cannot reproduce."

You look around. You see a light shining upon a man near the front. He is standing about fifty rows of people back from the platform. The man has fair skin, light brown hair that is trimmed shorter than his ears, straight lips, gentle eyes, long ears, and a slightly pointed nose. The man looks up toward Moses with a knowing confidence.

With a smile and an inviting gesture with his staff, Moses says, "Come forward, Clive Staples Lewis."

The entire place radiates with liveliness and joy as the man moves toward the platform. Love emanates from the crowd toward this man. You do not know this man's significance, yet you also feel an affection toward him. He is highly celebrated and loved by the inhabitants of heaven.

Moses steps back and gives Clive center stage. "Thank you for your willingness to serve the Lord this day in the temple courts. We all await the wisdom the Lord has imparted to you. Speak, for we are listening."

Clive steps to the center of the platform and bows low out of respect for the people of God. "Thank you, citizens of the King, for hearing me this day," Clive begins. His voice has a mellow, thoughtful tone.

You are struck by how different the presence of this man is from that of Moses. Yet, despite their differences, each man carries a depth within them that draws your attention. Clive's stance appears less bold than that of Moses, yet you feel the authority he carries to speak of the deep things of the Lord.

Clive introduces a series of thoughts for all to consider.

> "People of light, I will now demonstrate to you how liberty can lead to separation."

An image—one that is fully visible to the mind yet not fully visible to the eye—fills the Inner Courts. The image shows a great Lion next to a child. The child is chained to the Lion. As the Lion moves, the child's feet are forced to follow the Lion's motion. The Lion then begins to cut the chains with His teeth. He bites the chains until they break.

Clive interprets the scene.

> "This child represents each of us. The Lion represents our Lord. Our Lord does not chain us to Him."

The scene continues. The Lion runs up a hill. When He reaches the top, He turns back and looks at the child. The child runs toward the Lion. This time, the child is not chained to the Lion. The child runs to the Lion out of love.

Clive speaks again:

> "There is a special love that lives in liberty. Without liberty, this love would not exist. Without liberty, we would be chained to God."

As you watch Clive speak, you feel his energy, which communicates wisdom, love, and curiosity all at once.

Clive continues:

> "I ask you a question, citizens of heaven. Ponder this question, and do not push it aside. For within it is a mystery. Why didn't God make us perfect from the beginning? God is perfect. Why not make

us more like Himself? Isn't perfection better than imperfection? Isn't it better for perfect love to be guaranteed forever than for there to be the risk of imperfect love, or no love at all?"

Clive postures himself with one arm reaching across his midsection and the other arm folded upward toward his chin. He closes his eyes. By doing so, he invites the multitude to enter into a state of reflection and deep thought.

You can tell that this sort of reflection is not new to this man. This line of questioning lies within well-trodden territory for Clive. You can sense the meticulousness by which he has explored each rock and crevice and blade of grass. No rock or tree is foreign. There is much wisdom that this man, Clive, has gleaned from this sort of deep reflection.

Clive emerges from his deep thought and swipes his hand across the air, clearing the image that had appeared previously. Once Clive lowers his hand, the atmosphere of the Inner Courts is filled with pure light. The light grows brighter and brighter, until all you see everywhere is pure white light. You see no one else. You do not even see yourself. All you see is the light.

You hear the familiar voice of the Lord:

*"I am in all things. I am
perfection. Apart from me,
there is no perfection. Where
there is perfection, I am
there."*

The light then fades, and the multitude in the Inner Courts come back into view.

Moses steps to the center of the platform beside Clive. He puts his hand on Clive's shoulder and encourages him to speak.

Clive goes on to interpret the experience of the light:

"The Lord is in all things. He is Perfection. All that is perfect is contained within Him. If God only allows perfection, there is no distinction, and there is no creation. Therefore, creation entails that a creature is not Perfection in its identity."

Clive straightens his posture and extends his hands warmly. He continues:

"But, as an imperfect creature, you have been given the gift of liberty. You have been granted the power to cling to the perfection in God. Thus, we all have the power to pull His Perfection into us by inviting God into our experience. In this way, we can all be perfect. While we are distinct from Perfection, we can partner with Perfection. We are kingly creatures, who have the power of liberty to separate ourselves from the foundation of all perfection, or to rule and reign in the Lord's Perfection. Citizens of heaven, you have chosen to rule and reign with the Lord!"

Moses stands by Clive's side with approval. Moses lifts his hands into the air. He addresses the multitude:

"The more you see, the clearer the path. If any person is uncertain about anything, that person should seek more wisdom. Wisdom brings light."

Moses turns to Clive. "Thank you, my son, for sharing wisdom of the Lord with grace and a humble heart. We have benefited greatly from your insight."

Moses opens his arms, and Clive and Moses embrace. After a moment, Clive bows again to the multitude and exits the platform.

Moses turns to the fourth pillar, which is to his right side, slightly before him. He points his staff toward the fourth pillar. The pillar begins to glow, with a sparkling mist swirling around it. All four pillars sparkle now, living with energy.

Moses speaks to the pillar: "Open!"

The fourth pillar opens. Again, there is a scroll inside. Again, a white cloud rolls onto the temple floor. The scroll glows with an intense glow.

Moses speaks to the scroll: "Wisdom, come forth!" However, the glow stays tightly around the scroll. It does not reach out to him as did the wisdom of the previous scrolls.

Moses raises an eyebrow slightly. He speaks again, but with a deeper voice: "Wisdom, come forth!"

Again, nothing happens.

You can see that Moses is surprised and is pondering what to do.

Then, slowly, the glow surrounding the scroll begins to unwind. It swirls outward, ever so minutely. Moses focuses his attention on the scroll. He gazes into it, drawing from its wisdom. The glow gently and slowly makes its way to Moses. It appears as though it moves by Moses' intent to draw it near, yet it moves with some sort of resistance.

Everyone waits for Moses to speak.

While still facing the scroll, Moses says with a quiet voice, "I have not seen the wisdom of this scroll before."

Moses' eyes are transfixed upon the scroll. You can sense that Moses is learning as he gazes into it. The time during which Moses is captivated by the scroll and its contents feels brief in duration but deep in experience.

Moses is shining with a light that contains many colors. The light has new depth that has not been present until now. Moses' zeal is strong, but it is tempered with great humility.

Moses announces to the multitude,

> "The name of this pillar is *Agreements*. Inside this pillar, I see ancient wisdom that existed before the human story began."

Moses begins to reveal the ancient wisdom from the pillar of Agreements to the heavenly audience. Here is what he says:

> "The wisdom in love abounds and abounds. No eye has seen the limits of the wisdom of love. In this wisdom, the Lord has made arenas for many beings to

discover many things. Every arena has laws.

"Do you know what a law is? A law is an agreement.

"Before all stories, God made an agreement with Himself to make a world of worlds. Each world is a place for great things to emerge. To achieve many of these great things, God makes contracts with souls. God places these souls in worlds according to agreements between God and souls. No soul enters a world without consent."

Moses pauses again, as if deep in thought. After a moment of reflection, he continues:

"Some souls consent to a hero's journey. In the hero's journey, there are real stakes. There is real risk. Heroes rise in the soil of uncertainty.

"Our Lord makes contracts with these souls before they take any form or enter any world."

Moses lifts up his face and prays to the Most High. "Who are these heroic souls, Lord?"

Moses' eyes suddenly become wide, and then they fill with tears.

Moses faces the multitude. Wiping away his tears, he gazes into the eyes of many standing throughout the temple courts. Lifting his staff toward the multitude, he says,

> "Many of us here are heroes of old. This knowledge has been hidden from ages past, before our stories began."

Determination crosses Moses' face. He now speaks boldly:

> "Kings and queens of the Inner Courts, we have so much light now. The light makes the path obvious to all who love truth. How is the Lord's question to us even a test? By God's grace, we have more wisdom than we need. If there is any remaining doubt about how we must answer the Lord's question, that doubt is the minimum necessary doubt for there to be any remaining test."

Moses scans the multitude and rests his gaze on Adam. He calls, "Adam, do you now see why we cannot offer a separated soul a place with us? We have no right. All souls made an agreement to abide by the terms of the world in which they entered. Thus, all souls who separated themselves from God's light are under contract to be separated. They agreed to their contract. As surely as we cannot break the Lord's throne, we cannot break the Lord's agreements. No one can."

With outstretched arms, Moses boldly delivers a summary of his case. He deliberately points his staff as he speaks.

> "These pillars contain the wisdom of the Lord, which has endured throughout the ages. The pillars rest upon a foundation of love.
>
> "Wisdom defines the order of love. From wisdom, we can see that love requires that separated souls must remain separated. For if they are not separated, there is no justice, God's revelation is not trustworthy, there is no liberty, and the agreements made in the Lord's presence are broken."

Moses lowers his hands. He then kneels before everyone and lays down his staff. Moses gently lifts up his face and asks, "Are we now ready to answer the Lord's question?"

CHAPTER FOUR

The Hopeful Speak

MOSES' QUERY invites the thoughts and feelings of the multitude to surface. Everyone in the Inner Courts feels the strength of the case of the Noble, but opinions diverge concerning whether the case is ready to be closed. You pick up the thought impressions of many of those around you:

> "What else can be said?"

> "The wisdom of the pillars has
> been revealed."

> "The case of the Noble is too
> strong to answer."

"Adam has yet to present the case of the Hopeful... How will he reply?"

"We cannot yet answer the Lord's question, for we have yet to hear Adam speak."

The thoughts begin to converge into a swirling ball of colors. As the swirling colors coalesce, you hear a voice within you say, "Invite the Hopeful to speak."

You turn your heart toward the representative of the Hopeful. Energy leaps from you toward the epicenter of the Hopeful crowd. The flow of energy increases as everyone across the Inner Courts directs their invitation toward the man, Adam. The energy combines with the swirling colors of the thoughts and questions of the multitude and pours over the representative of the Hopeful.

Adam glows brightly. The energy condenses into an armor of light and permeates Adam's being, and this greatly emboldens Adam. Everyone in the Inner Courts cheers as they welcome Adam to the platform. With grace and excitement, Adam approaches the platform where Moses is kneeling.

Adam looks quite different than Moses. Adam is more decorated and appears more carefree. You have the sense that the appearances of the two men diverge in accordance with their unique personalities and dispositions.

Adam's hair is as black as ebony. It lies in tight, short spirals across his head, forming rows of black. He wears no hair on his face or chin. Adam's face, which is slightly darker than Moses' face, is sleek and strong, with defined cheekbones under his dark eyes. His nose is sleek and curved, and his lips are full. He wears a loose-fitting shirt that is tied close around his waist, and pants that extend barely to the knee. His outfit is white, with a belt of gold. He also wears various golden ornaments over his ears and around his neck, arms, ankles, wrists, and fingers. His expression is almost giddy.

Adam trots up the steps and walks lightly over to Moses. He puts his right hand on Moses' head and says, "May the Lord bless you, my son! Well done! We are all thankful for your humble service and great wisdom, which comes to you from the Lord."

Adam steps back and gestures with both hands toward Moses. Moses stands to his feet and gives a low bow.

Moses says to Adam, "Thank you for your blessing. May the Lord ever increase you with His abundance! It is an honor to serve the Lord and His people in this place. Now, we await your wisdom, firstborn of our people."

Moses steps to the side and gestures toward Adam.

"Please, Moses. Sit!" Adam invites with a bow.

Adam raises his hand, and as he does, a beautifully ornamented golden chair grows up from the floor near the edge of the platform.

Moses nods graciously. He retreats toward the decorated chair. His gait lacks any hint of hastiness or doubt. A thought enters you: "He is a noble man, indeed." Moses sits down in the golden chair. He looks expectantly at Adam.

Adam steps to the center of the platform. He puts out his hand, and a glowing scepter appears within it. He points the scepter to the ground and speaks, *"Bara!"*

Suddenly, a tree grows up from the middle of the platform. Moses looks somewhat startled. The tree grows thick and tall and wide, and its many branches reach to the edges of the Inner Courts. Buds appear on the tree. The buds grow into bright flowers, pink on the inside and white on the edges. The flowers then close. In their place, tiny fruit begins to grow. The fruit grows larger until it reaches maturity. The fruit sparkles.

Adam pulls some fruit off the tree.

The thought forms in your mind: "What is the meaning of this fruit? Is this new wisdom?" You are not sure whether this thought has originated from you or if you have picked it up from the minds of people around you.

Adam bites into the fruit. He is smiling as he eats.

Adam looks out toward the people in the temple. "Want some?" he asks with a chuckle.

Upon Adam's words, the tree bends. The branches of the tree reach downward toward the multitude below so that the people can reach pieces of fruit for themselves.

A branch descends in front of you. A piece of fruit sparkles before you. You reach up and pick the fruit, which detaches effortlessly from the branch. The fruit is soft and golden. It has a somewhat round, yet pointed shape.

You begin to eat the fruit. It tastes sweet, and a tad spicy. As you swallow, a feeling of gladness fills you completely.

Adam exchanges a glance with Moses. Moses looks back with fruit in hand. His eyes are inquisitive. Adam chuckles.

Then Adam turns to the crowd and speaks:

> "Moses is right that the wisdom in love abounds and abounds. No eye has seen the limits of the wisdom of love."

Adam looks back toward the tree. He points his scepter to the ground again, slightly to the left of the tree. The ground rumbles. Out from the platform, a stone—larger and taller than Adam—emerges. The stone is somewhat jagged, with many crevices.

Moses leans in his chair to inspect the stone, which has arisen on the opposite side of the platform.

With fruit still in hand, Adam points his scepter toward the stone. The stone shimmers and glows with radiant light.

Adam looks out over the faces of the citizens of heaven. He announces,

> "This stone is called *Hidden Treasure.*"

Adam faces the stone. He peers carefully into one of the crevices in the front face of the stone. Placing his scepter under one arm, he reaches into the crevice and pulls something out. It is a small scroll.

Adam turns back to the crowd. With a gentle flick of the wrist, Adam unrolls the small scroll.

He holds it up, reading it to himself. Then he turns the scroll around so that the multitude can see the contents.

The scroll has but a single line written across the middle of it.

Adam calls in a loud voice:

> "Hear, oh kings and queens of heaven, what is written on the scroll!"

He turns the scroll toward himself once more and reads:

> *"It is the glory of God to conceal a matter; to search out a matter is the glory of kings."*

Adam takes another bite of his fruit and rolls up the scroll in his hand. He walks over to Moses, who is sitting comfortably. Adam hands the scroll to Moses.

Moses accepts the scroll. He inspects every detail.

Adam addresses the multitude, with his fruit still in one hand and his scepter under his arm:

> "Friends, there is always more to discover. There is always more to see. Some treasures are hidden in secret places so that kingly creatures will seek

them out. There are many more treasures to see. There are treasures no eye has ever seen."

Adam takes a relaxed posture and begins to pace across the stage. He maintains a smile while he is deep in thought. He begins to speak, often looking down, while remaining completely attuned with his audience:

"The secrets of God are revealed in the stories of life. Long ago, in the story of my life, the Lord placed me into a beautiful garden that He had prepared for me. He assigned me the joy of tending to that beautiful place. But after a short time, I was cast out of paradise because I sinned greatly.

"I felt immense shame. I felt alone. I felt lost. Oh, how I longed to go back to the garden of God!

"But I did not yet understand that God was going to use even my fall for a great purpose. After I lost my glorious garden, my job was to create new gardens for myself and my family. I had to work by the sweat of my brow in thorny ground. My eyes could not see at that time what God had in mind to do.

"My new assignment was much harder because of my sin. The new ground had many thorns and thistles. Often, good plants would shrivel up and die. My hands would bleed from blisters and thorn pricks as I labored to create a good garden.

"Every prick of a thorn reminded me of my shame. This place of toil was judgement against me. The pain reminded me of the punishment I deserved.

"What I didn't see at the time was a treasure buried in my punishment. My punishment was part of a greater process. During my experience on the earth, while living under a curse, I learned to separate good from evil, thorns from flowers, and wise thoughts from foolish ones. My pain was part of a process that was changing me from the inside out. God was cultivating a new garden inside of my heart.

"Although I mourned the loss of paradise, my new assignment taught me to overcome problems and to develop new virtue. The Lord grew special fruit from the soil of my trouble. I gained new powers, new wisdom, and new virtues to lead others. I also gained a new understanding of good and evil, and how to recognize the patterns of darkness that can come into every soul."

Adam stops. He is no longer grinning—no, not at all. His expression has turned rather solemn. He speaks in a low voice,

"My dear children, let me ask you: do souls serve justice? Or does justice serve souls?"

The multitude awaits Adam's answer. "Is he waiting for us to reply?" you wonder.

After a moment, Adam turns to Moses and looks deep into Moses' eyes. Adam's face is as straight and serious as you have ever seen it. Adam repeats his question, this time addressing Moses alone. "Do souls serve justice, or does justice serve souls?"

Moses merely blinks, without saying anything.

Adam turns again to the multitude. His face relaxes. With a familiar smile, he says:

"Listen, my dear cherished ones. Many mysteries are unraveled in the experience of your lives. There are more

> truths revealed in a life than in a
> thousand books."

Adam takes up the scepter again in his right hand. He waves the scepter before him. An immense translucent image appears in front of Adam, before the multitude. In the image, boys are playing near a river. A man with a staff comes to the boys. The man shouts, "Kids, come away from the river." The boys stop their play. The man continues, "Listen to me. That river is rough. I don't want you to fall into the river. Please come play over by the hills instead."

The image pauses.

Adam points to the image and says,

> "The man has given his children an instruction to protect them. Will they listen? Suppose they do not. Suppose his children continue to play near the river. What will the man do then? What would you do if you were the man?"

The motion of the image continues where it left off. The boys continue to play next to the river. The man with the staff runs to the boys and shouts, "Come boys, it is time to go home." The man picks up both boys, one in each arm. He carries the boys away from the river and onto a path home. "You can't play here anymore," he says.

The translucent image vanishes.

Adam says,

> "Throughout the course of a life, there are times to give correction. The purpose of correction is to protect and help a life. But how do you correct a kingly creature?"

Adam closes his eyes and breathes in deeply. You sense that he is drawing upon the Lord's strength and wisdom. As he does, he begins to glow with brilliant colors.

Adam sweeps his scepter in front of him. The translucent image appears again. This scene takes us once more to the boys by the river. The sky in the scene is darker this time. Their father warns, "Kids, come away from the river." The boys disregard their father. This time the man yells, "You have disrespected my authority!"

The man waves his staff in the air. On the staff, a word burns in fiery letters: "REVENGE." The man begins to beat the boys with his staff. The boys cry out in pain.

As the boys are crying, the man says, "Serves you right!"

You hear gasps throughout the temple. Boos spread throughout the crowd.

Adam nods his head in affirmation. He says reassuringly,

> "Yes, dear children, by the guiding light within our hearts, all of us here know the wrongness of revenge. Revenge is not justice. Revenge is a distortion of justice. Revenge is a product of hate, not love. By the light within you, you see that revenge does not fulfill the requirements of justice."

Adam scans his eyes across the multitude. He asks everyone,

> "What are the requirements of justice?"

The multitude replies in unison, "Tell us, Adam, what you see."

Adam smiles. He continues,

> "Let me tell you a great secret. This secret is recorded inside the book of every heart."

Adam points his scepter toward Moses' heart. As he pulls his scepter back, a red ribbon emerges from Moses' chest and weaves its way into the air. On the ribbon is lots of tiny golden writing. Moses appears puzzled and intrigued.

Adam explains:

"In the heart of Moses is wisdom about justice. The purposes of justice and punishment are written on his heart. These purposes are written on every heart. Check your own hearts, and see if what I am saying is right.

"I declare to you the purposes of justice I see. One purpose of justice is to protect. In the first scene, when the man with the staff carried his boys away from the river, he restricted their play. This restriction is a type of punishment. It is a punishment that protects. Some punishment protects people from themselves and from others.

"There are other purposes in justice. When I was cast out of paradise, the consequences of my sin forged inside of me greater wisdom, virtue, and understanding. My punishment molded me into a new person. I was transformed by the fire of life. I was also being prepared to rule vastly greater realms—

realms much greater than I could dream of at the time.

"Please understand, my children. There are many forms of justice. But these forms are not hidden behind clouds of mystery. By the Lord's light, you can see the virtues of justice right inside your own hearts.

"Behold a great truth inside you: justice is served when people are served. *Justice serves souls.* Justice protects souls. Justice purifies souls. Justice prepares souls for greater things.

So I ask you, how does justice serve a soul who becomes separated from life itself? If the Lord knew a soul would become separated, why create that soul? Can the Lord create a soul without *a good end?*"

Adam then points to the first pillar called Justice.

"Moses is right that dark souls deserve separation. But is their separation the end of their story? Or could their very separation serve a greater purpose, just as my separation from the Garden of Eden served a greater purpose?

"Here is my response to Moses' first argument, which is the argument from justice. His argument is incomplete. By the Lord's light, we agree that true justice is not revenge. The purpose of justice is good, while the purpose of revenge is not good. *Permanent separation* is not good. So, permanent separation cannot be the purpose of justice. If a soul must remain separated, it is for another reason."

Adam walks from center stage to where Moses is seated in the golden chair. Adam bends over and looks Moses in the eyes. A smile crosses Adam's face, and without any warning, he grabs Moses' beard! Moses' eyes widen. Adam gives the beard a quick, gentle tug, and then releases his grip. To everyone's surprise, a small, yet thick, scroll rolls out of Moses' beard and comes to rest on his lap.

"May I?" Adam asks, as he extends his hand toward Moses. Moses picks up the scroll and hands it to Adam. You detect no feelings of offense within Moses—only curiosity and love.

Adam looks up toward the multitude and says,

"Let us look now at Moses' second argument, which is the argument from revelation."

Adam walks back to center stage, points down at the scroll in his hand, and announces to the multitude,

"This scroll contains revelation given to the Hebrews and the Gentiles. In this revelation are layers of understanding. Some things are easy to understand, while others contain meaning that kings of old have still not fully grasped. *Meanings are unlocked by experience.* To unlock a fuller range of meaning in this revelation requires a fuller range of experience."

Adam opens the scroll and gazes upon its contents. After a moment, he points his finger to a particular passage in the scroll. He then raises his scepter. A translucent image again appears in the air before him and the multitude. The image shows a large fish swallowing a man.

Adam says,

"This man is Jonah. The scroll in my hands records the time of Jonah's being trapped in the fish. How long was he trapped? The scroll says *forever*." (See Jonah 2:6, Septuagint.)

Adam raises his scepter and points in midair. The word "FOREVER" appears in gold.

Adam then asks,

"What is the meaning of 'forever'? Does forever have an end?"

He looks upon the multitude with love and understanding.

"I humbly suggest that your understanding of 'forever' will depend on the experiences you have had in your life up until the point when you hear the word 'forever.' Your experiences give you your interpretation."

As the creatures in the temple ponder Adam's words, a dense fog rolls out from the platform where Adam stands. The fog expands until it surrounds every being in the temple. The fog makes it difficult to see very far across the temple floor, but the air above remains clear. Above the fog, Adam remains clearly visible in your sight.

Adam points at the fog. "This fog represents a mystery. There is something here that we have yet to grasp."

Lifting up the scroll in his hands, Adam continues:

> "The scroll tells us that the fish spits out the man after three days. So we see that Jonah's time in the fish had an end. This forever was *not endless*. May our experience with this scroll give us insight."

The holographic image changes to a scene of sheep and goats, who are being separated by a shepherd.

Adam points toward Moses.

> "Moses told us that the goats are separated from the sheep forever. I tell you, what this noble man has told us is indeed true."

The word "FOREVER" glistens again in the air. Adam continues:

> "But I ask you, could this forever have an end? Your answer depends on the experience that fills your mind when you hear the word 'forever'. Pay attention to

the meaning of the word. This word, 'forever,' is the same as the word that describes Jonah's time in the fish. Jonah's forever had an end. So, let me ask you: could the separation of goats likewise come to an end?"

Adam turns his eyes to the side as if in thought. He recounts:

"When I was banished from the Garden of Eden, I was separated from paradise. I could not turn back if I tried. I lost a great treasure that I could never get back. Yet, here I am with you in this great place. I am among great treasures. The steps of time have led me into a greater place than I ever knew. What I lost in ages past has now been restored to me in even greater measure."

Adam looks again at the scroll that had emerged from Moses' beard. Adam unrolls it a bit. He says joyfully,

"Look! There is something amazing, and possibly strange, written in this scroll. What I am about to share with you will affect you in accordance with the experiences you've had until this moment."

Adam clears his throat and announces,

"Our Lord has said, 'I tell you the truth, all the sins of the sons of men shall be forgiven.'" (See Mark 3:28.)

Adam looks toward Moses. Moses scrunches his eyebrows. Adam asks Moses, "Great man of wisdom, what do you think these words mean? When our Lord says that 'all the sins of the sons of men shall be forgiven,' what could that mean? Could it mean that *all the sins of the sons of men shall be forgiven?*" There is no sarcasm in Adam's voice. He is humble, but playful.

Without waiting for Moses to respond, Adam turns to the multitude and says, "My dear children, your understanding of these words depends on the experiences that fill your mind when you hear these words."

Moses lifts his hand to indicate his desire to speak. Adam smiles and places a piece of fruit into Moses' hand.

Adam says to Moses, "You have many good thoughts and questions on your mind. I feel them. I see them. All good things will come into the light in their proper time. In the meanwhile, enjoy this fruit. You'll like it."

With patience and peace, Moses leans back in his chair. He smiles and takes a bite of the fruit. Moses is so happy and full of love, in fact, that his eyes are glistening. Moses agrees to wait before raising his response.

Adam looks across the multitude and locks eyes with a woman. "If Moses will invite a guest onto his stage, then I will as well," Adam says. "Xie Daoyun, will you join me?"

A small woman begins to make her way to the platform. She is wearing ornamented silk robes, white in color, embroidered with red and gold flowers. There is a golden sash around her waist. She has fair skin and black eyes. Her sleek black hair is artistically wrapped on top of her head. Many gold, jeweled hair pins stud her hair. A large golden ornament is embedded into her hair at the crest of her head. The ornament looks like a rising sun. Golden picks cross through her wrapped hair, the ends of which peek out on the sides of her head like golden sun rays. She walks briskly and gracefully.

"This woman is gifted with both insight and artistic skills," says Adam.

Adam looks toward Daoyun with kindness and admiration. He says, "Daoyun, while we have been talking, a poem has formed in your spirit. What you have created could benefit us all. Will you please share your poem with us?"

"Yes, certainly," Daoyun replies in a quiet, courteous voice. She stands up straight and folds her hands. She then recites her poem:

> *Soul is sleeping*
> *Bowl is heaping*
> *Danger leaping*
> *Anger seeping*
> *Ever reaping*
> *Ever weeping*
> *Never keeping*
> *Never sleeping*

The small woman bows after reciting the poem.

Adam looks at Daoyun and asks, "Daoyun, may I ask you about this poem?"

She nods.

"What soul is sleeping, Daoyun?" Adam asks.

Daoyun replies, "This is the soul that has departed from the Eternal Spirit."

"Why is the bowl heaping?" Adam asks.

"The weight of karma is heavy for the sleeping soul," the woman replies. "That is why danger is always springing out of nowhere, and why the soul is angry. But the soul will continue to bear the effects of karma as long as it is sleeping."

"Is that why there is weeping?" Adam asks.

"Yes," the woman answers. "The sleeping soul weeps. The Eternal Spirit also weeps."

"How do you interpret the last two lines of your poem, Daoyun?" asks Adam.

"There are two interpretations possible," Daoyun explains. "One is this. If the Eternal Spirit does not sustain the sleeping soul, that sleeping soul will never again rest. The torment of that soul will continue forever apart from the Eternal Spirit."

"And what is the second?" Adam asks.

"The second is this," the woman says. "The Eternal Spirit never keeps love from the sleeping soul. The bowl one day becomes empty. The sleeping soul awakens, never to sleep again."

Adam nods. He reflects on the poem and ponders its interpretations. "Thank you, Daoyun, for your wisdom." He bows in respect to her. She bows, then returns to the crowd.

Adam once more directs his attention to the multitude:

"Treasures leave clues. Not every treasure is obvious right away. Some treasures require many experiences to unlock. It is the glory of kings to search out these treasures. There is always more to see.

"Listen, my friends. Moses is right about the wisdom of the pillars. As Moses has shown us, the pillars of Justice and Revelation together testify to the need for separation. There must indeed be a separation. There must be a separation between sheep and goats, good and evil, citizens of heaven and agents of darkness. Therefore, there *is* separation. The darkest souls are indeed separated from us. We can attest to this separation by our own experience.

"But our vision is limited. Do we see how long this separation must be? Must separation be endless? I have searched many scrolls, many hearts, and many lives, and I have seen many speculations and many wise arguments. But I have never seen any clock that tells the timing of separation. The timing of separation has not been made clear to me.

"On the contrary, in the records of the many lives I've encountered, I find hints of a greater hope. There are hints of plans to restore what was lost.

"Here, then, is my response to Moses' second argument, the argument from revelation. This argument is also incomplete. We saw that the word 'forever' describes Jonah's time in the fish. That time was not endless. It came to an end when Jonah came out of darkness. So could the separation of a soul likewise come to an end? So far, Moses has not demonstrated from divine revelation that the timing of separation must go on without end. Yes, there is more to consider. But the light we have seen here still leaves room for hope.

"I ask you, citizens of the kingdom, why close a door if the Lord has not closed it?"

Adam then points his scepter to the pillar called Liberty.

"I now want to address Moses' argument from liberty. We have heard that liberty is part of love. Liberty is indeed part of love. But could too much liberty break love?"

An image appears once again in the air and displays a new scene. A girl is running toward a cliff. Her father shouts, "Stop!" The girl continues to run toward the cliff. The father sprints quickly after her. As she approaches the edge, the girl stops and faces her father. He stops as well.

The father says to the girl, "It's your choice, my beloved daughter. You can walk toward me, or you can back away from me."

The father watches as the girl begins taking steps backward toward the cliff. Step. Step. Step.

After another step, the girl falls over the edge of the cliff. She screams as she falls, down and down. The father keeps his distance from the edge, looking away from where his daughter had fallen. The scene then shows the girl as she is falling. To her great horror, the pit has no bottom.

As she falls, terror and torment overwhelm her. She falls for one day, two days, three days, one month, one year, one hundred years. She is fully conscious and terrified day and night as she falls. She will never stop falling, forever and ever.

A deathly silence overcomes everyone in the temple. It is not frequently that the thoughts of the citizens of heaven are drawn to consider the horrors that face separated souls.

Adam breaks the silence with an interpretation of the image of the girl displayed in the Inner Courts.

"My dear sons and daughters, there are some liberties love could never grant you. It is written, "Love always protects." How could I protect you, my children, if I allowed you to fall into a bottomless pit? Could I allow you to completely destroy yourselves forever, without any chance of rescue? I couldn't. My love for you could not allow that."

Adam turns to Moses. Moses is gazing into the distance, deep in thought. As Adam's feelings of love land upon Moses, Moses focuses his eyes on Adam's eyes.

"Moses, my son, you are wise," Adam says, "but you are also much younger than I. Your love is not filled up with as many episodes of experience. My love for you is vast and dense. If you could fully comprehend all my love for you, you would know that I could never take the risk of permitting your endless ruin. I would always make a way for you to return. I would never give up on you. I would never let you go."

Moses' eyes are wet with tears.

Adam addresses the multitude once more:

"Here, citizens of heaven, is why I cannot accept Moses' third argument, the argument from liberty. This argument, like the others, is incomplete. Moses is right that love grants liberty. But this same liberty keeps hope alive. If my child runs away from home, I will always hope they return. Yes, I will grant my child liberty, to protect them from being controlled, but not to prevent them from being restored. So, if love indeed grants liberty, why couldn't some separated soul be granted the liberty *to be restored?* Liberty leaves open the possibility for restoration."

Adam then points to the fourth pillar, which is called Agreements. Instead of giving an analysis, he remarks:

"These agreements are very interesting and very strange. I must say, I do not quite know what to say about them. I don't trust them. There is something off about the whole idea. Why would souls like us ever agree to such high stakes? Would any kingly creature agree to risk everlasting torment if they fully understood the stakes? Why would the Lord risk the loss of a child if there were no backup plan to restore that child? And why don't I remember signing these agreements? These agreements are mysterious to me."

Adam's response sparks questions in you. "Is Adam questioning one of the pillars of wisdom? Does Adam lack an answer to Moses' argument from agreements? How can the multitude in the Inner Courts see what is true if even Adam can't see what is true?"

The white fog in the temple is now thick. The fog almost covers over the heads of the multitude. The feeling of uncertainty lingers in the atmosphere.

You hear a quiet voice inside you say,

"Mystery is an invitation to discover treasure."

Upon hearing these words, joy and peace fill your being. You have a deep sense that something great is waiting to be revealed.

Adam addresses the multitude:

"My friends, there are many things we do not understand. Let us be careful not to fill in an understanding we do not have. When we do not see, *we do not see.*

"I tell you, Noble and Hopeful citizens of heaven, I do *not see* that every single separated soul must remain separated. The pillars of Justice, Revelation, Liberty, and Agreements give me no such sight. In the pillar of Justice, I see that justice serves souls, but I do *not see* that justice must serve a soul with endless separation. In the pillar of Revelation, I see that an age of separation can come to an end, just as Jonah's time in the fish came to an end. But I do *not see* that every soul who is now separated from us must remain separated for an age with no end. In the pillar of Liberty, I see that love places boundaries on liberty, but I do *not see* that a separated soul cannot still be granted the liberty to be restored. In the pillar of Agreements, I see nothing but mist. So, I do *not see* that every separated soul must remain separated. Hope remains alive."

Adam then faces Moses squarely and asks gently, "Moses, does your wisdom have room for hope?"

CHAPTER FIVE

The Great Dialogue

YOU BEHOLD the two wise souls, Adam and Moses, on the platform. Adam stands, looking at Moses intently. Moses is sitting, stroking his beard. The two are invested in making their respective cases, yet they also feel great empathy for one another.

You feel the weight of the question being discussed. *Can a separated soul be given a body of life?* In the midst of tension, the love of the Lord permeates the room. You feel connected in spirit to both the Noble and the Hopeful.

Moses stops stroking his beard and looks up at Adam. "Is it my time to speak?" he asks quietly, leaning in and whispering only to Adam. (All who desire to hear this quiet whisper can hear it by simply focusing intently on Moses' lips.)

Adam beckons Moses, saying, "Join me now. Let us talk openly with one another."

Moses stands to his feet. He begins to walk toward the center of the platform. Meanwhile, Adam pushes Moses' golden chair to the center. Once Moses reaches the center, Adam scoots the chair directly behind Moses and indicates for him to sit.

Adam then takes his scepter in hand and points it to the ground opposite Moses.

"Bara," Adam says with a smile.

Up from the platform arises another golden chair within sparkling mist. Looking amused, Adam sits triumphantly on the chair as he faces Moses.

As the two of them take their seats at center stage, the crowd sends waves of approval toward them both. They also send their thoughts, questions, and encouragement to both of them by the power of their intentions.

Adam addresses the multitude.

> "Listen, people of light! Moses has made a case for the Noble. I have made a case for the Hopeful. Now that the Noble and the Hopeful have spoken, we must

take time to interact with the concerns and questions that remain. We trust that the Spirit of the Lord will guide us as we continue our dialogue."

Adam turns back to Moses. "It is your turn to speak, my beloved son."

Moses says to Adam:

"My great father, thank you for sharing stories that provoke us to deep thought. I have many questions for you, however. My most pressing questions are about your interpretation of our Lord's revelation. There are many statements in the scrolls that seem to clearly show us the impossibility of forgiving those who are now separated from us. I have specific questions for you about specific passages. I am baffled as to how you do not see clearly what has been clear to so many of us. To be honest, Adam, I worry that your interpretations are guided by your desire, rather than by a serious understanding of the scrolls.

"When you read the scrolls, you interpret them with ideas outside the scrolls. You pull wisdom from strange places! You pull ideas from a crevice in a stone. You pull ideas from a ribbon in my heart. You even pull a scroll from my beard. How can we trust your sources?

"You pull wisdom from hearts and lives. But surely, Adam, hearts can mislead us. Our hearts always believe they are right. Yet our hearts can hope for things that are not true.

"If we are to see truth, must we not look beyond our own hearts? To know the truth, surely we must bow our hearts to the standards of reality revealed by our Lord. Don't you agree?"

Adam smiles and leans toward Moses. He asks, "How does the Lord reveal the standards of reality, Moses? Through scrolls?"

"Yes, scrolls and prophets. And pillars!" Moses says assertively.

"There are many scrolls, Moses," Adam replies lightly. "As you recall, I have retrieved scrolls from a stone and a beard. You have accessed scrolls inside heavenly pillars. So, tell me, Moses, are all scrolls equal? Is every scroll true? How do you know when a scroll is true?"

Moses answers without any delay, "When the Lord reveals a scroll, that scroll is true. The Lord cannot lie. The scrolls of the Lord are entirely true." He sits up slightly straighter now.

Adam's face straightens a bit to match Moses'. "Moses, how do you know when the Lord reveals a scroll? There are many scrolls throughout the universe. Could someone mistake a scroll of lies for a scroll from the Lord?"

Moses answers without a blink, "The Spirit of the Lord guides all souls. Lies cannot live in the presence of our Lord. Those who cling to the Lord are led by the Lord."

"You speak wisely," Adam replies. You can tell that Adam is pleased. "Yes, in the presence of the Lord, there is light. Light casts out darkness. When you are in the Light of Life, you see wisdom wherever the light touches."

Adam leans over and picks up the scroll that was on Moses' lap. Adam then holds it in the air. "If the Lord's light touches a scroll, you can see the wisdom in that scroll," says Adam.

Adam places the scroll back onto Moses' lap, and then Adam lightly touches his hand to the center of Moses' chest. "If the Lord's light touches your heart, Moses, then you can see wisdom in your heart."

Adam straightens his posture once more and concludes, "Without the light of the Lord, there is no wisdom. All wisdom begins in the Lord's light."

Moses has been watching Adam intently as Adam speaks. It appears to you that Moses finds Adam a bit unpredictable.

Moses looks down into his lap at the scroll. He looks back at Adam, eye to eye. "Yes, Adam, but wisdom doesn't end in the Lord's light. Wisdom takes a shape." Picking up the scroll, he adds, "Like the shape of a scroll or pillar."

"Do not think that I disagree with you, Moses," Adam clarifies. "I agree with you. Wisdom takes many shapes. Wisdom can take shape inside your heart. The light of the Lord can touch all things. When light comes into your heart, you can discern what is true, right, noble, and good." Adam's vocal tone and gestures are warm and assuring. "The Lord speaks to beings in many flavors and forms."

Adam waves his scepter into the air above him, and a translucent scene appears. In the scene, Adam is naming animals in the Garden of Eden.

Adam explains:

> "When I lived in the beautiful Garden of Eden, I was given the task of naming the animals. As the animals were

brought before me, I looked into their eyes. I saw unique potential inside each creature. I could feel the Creator's unique love for each animal, and out of that feeling of love, I gave each animal a name.

"I also had another task. The Lord invited me to communicate with the animals in accordance with their design. In this process, I learned that each animal has a unique way of understanding the voice of God inside it. The wisdom and messages of some creatures are simple, yet profound. The wisdom and messages of others contain more nuance and variety.

"As I mingled among the animals in the garden, I observed the Lord interact with His creatures. When the Lord spoke to a bee, the language was different than when He spoke to a lizard. He spoke in ways that mirrored the ways that His creatures spoke. The language of lizards is vastly different than the language of elephants or whales. The Lord speaks the language of the heart of His creatures, in accordance with their understanding.

"The Lord is so vast in wisdom. How can the same Lord who speaks to the eagle also speak to us? How can the same Lord who speaks to us also speak to the stars? I tell you, Moses, this vastness of the Lord is something that I do not yet grasp, even though I have been pondering it for many ages.

"I believe one reason the Lord wanted me to name the animals, and to learn their languages, is to better appreciate His magnificence. But another reason, I discovered, was to help me see my need for someone who can communicate in a language that is meaningful to me. No animal could fully comprehend or appreciate my own language, even though I could comprehend and appreciate theirs. The Lord knew that I needed to speak my heart language with others who would understand me. That is why, when no suitable companions could be found among the animals, the Lord took from my side a partner. This partner understood my heart language.

"I've learned from my experiences that the Lord speaks to every creature in unique ways they can understand. When the Lord speaks to the animals, He speaks to them in the language that brings them life. So, too, when the Lord speaks to humans, He speaks to each human in the language that brings them life. The Lord speaks to some by an inner light of reason, others by an artistic display, still others by a clever trail of clues."

Adam smiles. "When the Lord speaks to you, Moses, the Lord speaks with scrolls and pillars, because you love scrolls and pillars."

Moses lifts his eyebrows.

Adam turns again to the multitude. He then says enthusiastically, "While God's truth transcends all places and all things, his truth also takes unique forms in all places and in all things."

Moses leans in. He places one elbow on his knee and gestures with his hand as he talks. "Adam, if the Lord speaks in so many ways," Moses says, articulating his words slowly, "who can discern which way is right? What if the voice in someone's heart is inconsistent with the revelation in a scroll? Where will you find the truth then?"

"Let me ask you, Moses," Adam says gently, as he also leans in toward Moses, "how do you know what a scroll says? How do you unlock its meaning?"

Moses ponders the question briefly and then responds, "The meaning is given to us by the rules of language. Everyone can learn the rules of language and, with wisdom, anyone can decipher any scroll."

Adam leads Moses along by inquiring, "How do you decipher the rules of language? If you must know the meaning of the rules of language to unlock the meaning of the scrolls, how do you unlock the meaning of the rules of language?"

Moses pauses to consider his answer. His eyebrows lower in thought. Suddenly, his eyes widen as he lifts his head. He declares, "The Lord is the source of all meaning."

Adam's face straightens and he slumps back in his chair, as if slightly disappointed in Moses' answer. Adam raises his hand to his chin and rests his chin on the knuckle of one finger. "How does one know what the Lord says, Moses? How does one unlock the meaning of the Lord's voice?" Adam asks as he sits upright again.

Moses begins stroking his beard once more. You can tell that he is carefully examining his thoughts before a word leaves his mouth.

Before Moses speaks, Adam leans over and points to Moses' chest. Adam says, "The answer is in here—in your heart. In your heart, you experience meaning. Experience unlocks meaning. You cannot see any meaning without experience. Do you see, Moses? Without experience, you cannot understand any scroll. Your understanding of the scrolls cannot be separated from the experiences of your life."

Adam looks at Moses. Moses remains silent.

Adam continues,

> "Moses, you desire to protect us all from error. This desire is noble. In order to protect us, you point us to the pillars of wisdom, which contain the standards of reality. Yet, we can only be protected by seeing these pillars if we indeed *see these pillars*. How can we *see* the pillars of wisdom?
>
> "To see the pillars, we need light. To see anything, we need light. We need the Lord's light, for all light comes from the Lord. So, if there is a conflict between the wisdom contained within a heart and the wisdom contained within a scroll or pillar, we need the Lord's light to illuminate them both."

"Yes, Adam," says Moses in a serious tone. "We need the Lord in order to have any wisdom. He is the source of all wisdom. We need the light of the Lord."

Moses holds the scroll outward, between himself and Adam. He says, "Adam, the light of the Lord will illuminate the revelation contained inside this scroll. Let us only go forward with the light of the Lord."

Adam nods in agreement. "Yes, Moses. What you say is right. Let us consult the scroll with the Lord's light."

Moses nods in acknowledgement and opens the scroll. He points to some text and says,

"Look here, Adam. It is written by the prophet Daniel that at the end of the age, some souls go to everlasting life, while some go to everlasting destruction. We have seen with our own eyes the fulfillment of this prophecy. But you say that 'everlasting' can come to an end, just as Jonah's time in the fish came to an end. If you say that everlasting destruction can come to an end, will everlasting life also come to an end? Truth requires consistency. What is a consistent meaning of 'everlasting,' Adam?"

Adam smiles and replies, "Consistent? Why do you seek *consistency*, Moses?"

Moses, looking rather puzzled, explains, "Truth must be consistent. Can there be light where there is no light? Can there be truth where there is no truth? Surely not! Without consistency, everything is chaos."

Adam's smile persists while Moses speaks. Adam says cheerfully, "Ha! The light of the Lord is bright inside of you, Moses!"

Adam leans in toward Moses as he continues. Adam says, "When you see that truth is consistent, Moses, you see this truth by the Lord's light inside your mind. This light of the Lord is in every scroll from the Lord. This is the light of reason."

"Yes, Adam," Moses replies, "I am delighted that we do indeed agree. Truth must be consistent, as I have said before."

Moses lifts one hand in a non-confrontational manner. "But," Moses says gently, "you have not yet answered my question. What do you say about the Lord's scroll? What is the consistent meaning of 'everlasting'?"

Adam looks up, and two pieces of fruit fall from the overhanging tree branches into his lap. He chuckles, picking up the fruit. "Want another one?" he asks Moses.

Moses agrees, extending his hand to grab the fruit.

Adam holds the fruit up in his hand and looks at the fruit while he speaks. "You are not yet ready for my answer, Moses. First, you must understand something about the meaning of meaning. Listen carefully: meanings come in many different resolutions of detail."

Adam then looks at Moses and points to the fruit that Moses has just bitten into. "That fruit is great, isn't it, Moses?"

Moses lifts one eyebrow while he tastes the fruit in his mouth. "Why, yes, it is a great fruit, Adam. That is why I agreed to take another."

"Let me ask you, Moses," Adam continues. "Is the Lord's throne great?"

Almost in shock, Moses replies, "As certainly as I live, the greatness of the Lord's throne surpasses the greatness of all other thrones!"

Adam again points toward Moses' fruit. "You said that your fruit is great. You have also said that the Lord's throne is great. Both are great! But Moses, do tell me, what is the consistent meaning of 'great'?"

Moses appears thoughtful, but he is also filled with zeal. "There are many levels of greatness, Adam. My fruit, though very great indeed, cannot be compared with the greatness of the Lord's throne."

Adam nods and affirms, "True! Yet, both are great. How can both be great? Can we call your fruit and the Lord's throne 'great' in a single breath?"

Moses looks at his fruit. He then looks back at Adam. "You are asking me a strange question, Adam. Please, tell us what you see," Moses invites with an open gesture.

"Thank you," says Adam. He explains:

> "There is a general meaning of 'great'. This meaning is like a low-resolution image. Just as a low-resolution image doesn't fill in every detail, a low-resolution meaning doesn't fill in every detail. On a low-resolution meaning of greatness, we are not saying how great the fruit or the throne are. That is why we can call them both great in the same breath. The fruit and the throne both have some greatness. When you say that your fruit and the Lord's throne are

great, you are using a low-resolution meaning of 'great'.

"We are now ready to answer your question about the consistent meaning of 'everlasting'. This word describes a time that can come to an end, just as Jonah's time in the fish came to an end. Here also in the scroll, it is written, 'Edom's streams will be turned into pitch, her dust into burning sulfur; her land will become blazing pitch! It will not be quenched night or day; its smoke will rise forever.' (See Isaiah 34:9-10.)

"There is no smoke on Edom's streams today; the burning came to an end. The term 'forever', then, leaves open the time frame. We do not see from this word a high-resolution timeline specifying the length of time of the smoke on Edom's streams.

"Just as 'greatness' can have a meaning in low-resolution, so can the word 'everlasting'. Some scribes translate this word as 'age', since the word 'age' does not include a high-resolution meaning specifying the length of time. The scroll says, literally, that some go to an age of life, and others go to an age of destruction. It is tempting to fill in more meaning. But when you fill in meaning that is not in the scroll, you are filling in meaning from your own mind."

After a moment, Moses leans forward in his chair. He looks Adam in the eyes and says, "Let me make sure I understand what you are saying, Adam. You are saying that in this scroll, the Lord has left out the exact duration a soul will experience life or destruction. Is that right?"

"Precisely," says Adam.

Moses looks puzzled. He continues, "If I didn't know you better, Adam, I would weep. What you are saying doesn't add hope to souls. It subtracts hope from souls by removing assurance of everlasting life for all of us. Why would you suggest that, my beloved father?"

Those around you empathize with Moses.

"Moses," Adam says lovingly, "you know my heart toward you and toward all creatures. Have ears to hear what I am about to say. Do not let your hope sink."

Adam sits up straight and continues, "I have told you that the Lord reveals wisdom in many forms and flavors. The Lord reveals to our hearts that His love for us will uphold us. The Lord reveals hope in many places."

Adam motions to Moses. "May I?" asks Adam. Moses rolls up the scroll and hands it to Adam.

Adam opens the scroll and points to some text.

> "Listen, Moses! It is written on this scroll that the Lord clothes us with immortal bodies. As surely as our Lord is immortal, our lives, too, are immortal. Do not lose hope! The Lord will not forsake those to whom He has given everlasting life!
>
> "Remember, Moses, the reasons for hope are brighter in some places than in others. Just because one passage doesn't specify the age of life or death, that doesn't mean we cannot see from another passage that our life will go on without end."

Moses replies, "Let me review your argument. You have said that everlasting destruction may come to an end, just as Jonah's time in the fish came to an end. You have also said that 'everlasting' can envelop different time frames because its meaning can be low-resolution. You have argued that the life of the righteous ones will continue without end because they are given immortal bodies. I understand these points,

Adam. However, you have not considered everything in the scrolls."

Moses motions to Adam. Adam hands the scroll back to Moses. Moses opens the scroll and points. He says,

> "Look here, Adam. It is written that a great chasm separated the rich man in hell from Abraham and Lazarus in heaven. It is written that no one can cross the chasm. So, is it not clear? No separated soul can be given a place with us."

Adam replies without hesitation, "Many things that are impossible *now* are possible for our Lord *in time*. No one can cross the chasm between heaven and hell while that chasm exists. But must the chasm exist permanently? Perhaps our Lord has the power to make a bridge across the chasm. How can we rule out this possibility? In fact, as we saw, it is written that all the sins of the sons of men shall be forgiven. Remember that? So, perhaps some forgiveness for some souls will come after an age of separation."

Moses replies sharply, "But what about the unforgivable sin, Adam?"

Moses points down at the scroll.

"Look! Here it is written, 'whoever blasphemes against the Holy Spirit will never be forgiven; they are guilty of an eternal sin.' The words are plain. Never means never. Are you going to tell me that *never* doesn't mean *never?*"

Adam smiles. He asks, "Where does meaning come from, Moses? Does not your own experience create the meanings you associate with words?"

Adam then touches the text on the scroll and pulls his finger upward. Golden words appear above the scroll. The words are translated in your mind as follows:

'Whoever may speak evil in regard to the Holy Spirit hath not forgiveness for an age, but is in danger of age-enduring judgment.'

"These words," Adam points as he speaks, "represent another interpretation of this part of the scroll. The meaning of the words written here in gold above the scroll differs from the meaning of the words you have spoken, Moses. Different people, depending on their experiences, will read the scroll according to different interpretations.

"So, what if the meaning in someone's mind concerning what the scroll says is inconsistent with the meaning in someone else's mind? Where will you find the truth then?"

"In the scroll!" Moses declares.

Adam lowers his eyebrows. "Moses, we are already in the scroll! Yet, our minds can pull from the scroll different meanings. There is no meaning in the scroll without a mind. All meaning is in minds. Your mind has within it meaning that mine does not have. My mind has within it meaning that yours does not have. So, whose meaning is right?" Adam stares at Moses with sincerity and earnest.

"We must listen to the Lord, Adam," says Moses. "The meaning in the mind of the Lord is right, and true, and noble, and life-giving."

Adam presses, "But Moses, how can we know the mind of the Lord?" Adam leans in close. The edges of his lips squeeze closer together to form a serious look.

Moses brings his eyebrows together but says nothing.

Adam shares his reasoning with Moses:

"Our experiences unlock our understanding of the Lord's revelation. To have sight, we must have the Lord's light. Where we do not have light, we do not have sight.

"Let me tell you, Moses, what I see most clearly. By the Lord's light inside my heart, I see that love creates boundaries of protection. If you, Moses, ever began to slip down a pit, I would grab you, and I would not grant you the liberty to let go. I would always protect you. *Love always protects.*

"Does the pillar of Revelation tell us otherwise? Does it tell us that all hope is lost for every single soul who is now separated from us? The Lord's light does not give me that sight. Perhaps there is a child who has fallen down a pit of darkness, and he cannot escape on his own. Perhaps the Lord is waiting to see who will join Him in rescuing this separated child. Perhaps we are this child's only hope. Let not our partial sight of truth block us from seeing the possibility of a greater reality!"

Moses looks intently into Adam's eyes. After a long pause, Moses raises his eyebrows and says, "May the Lord increase the resolution of our understanding."

CHAPTER SIX

The King Speaks

SUDDENLY, in the distance, white clouds part to unveil a glorious throne, as wide as a hundred pillars and as tall as the sky. The throne is glowing so brilliantly that it appears white, but a spectrum of colors emerges from it. Upon the throne is seated a glorious being—the Eternal King. His body and face glow brighter than any sun. A majestic crown sits upon His head. His hair is golden. His robes are pure white. Love radiates from the throne and from the One seated upon it.

You feel immense power coming from the throne, even though the throne is beyond the Inner Courts by some significant distance.

"Behold! The Lord!" Adam announces. There is great reverence in the atmosphere. Many people bow low.

Moses and Adam turn toward the glorious throne behind them. Rainbows shine like brilliant halos all around the Eternal King. Together, Moses and Adam seek the Lord to unlock new depth of meaning. All the creatures in the Inner Courts gaze upon the glorious King, who sits on the throne.

You wonder, "Is this the true form of God?"

A quiet voice inside you replies, "God takes many forms, but God has no form. God is prior to all forms. God is eternal. God is the sustainer of all things that have form. Without God, no form would exist. No form—not even this grand form—can display the full power, love, and wisdom of the One from whom all things have their origin."

You look again at the King on the throne. You realize that this familiar voice inside you comes from the One on the throne. The voice has always felt so ordinary. Yet, in this moment, the voice seems special and grand.

All the people in the Inner Courts are wondering what the Lord will do. In the midst of the multitude, you experience many questions:

"What will the Eternal King
say?"

"Will the King say anything?"

"Will the King take the side of
the Noble?"

"Will the King take the side of
the Hopeful?"

"Will the King expose the error
of our thoughts?"

"Will the King reveal
something that has never
before been revealed?"

Suddenly, in the center of the platform
between Moses and Adam, a light appears. This
light is the light of the King on the throne.

Immediately, both Adam and Moses leave
their chairs and put their faces to the ground. All
the people throughout the temple also bow
before the light. You feel the awesomeness of the
presence of wisdom and love, and you descend to
your knees as well.

The light takes the shape of a man. He has a
gentle, plain face, shoulder-length brown hair,

and crystal blue eyes. He is wearing white robes. His aura glows brightly around his body.

As you gaze upon Him, you recognize His spirit. "This is the Lord," you say to yourself, with awe. The Lord touches Adam and Moses and says, "Stand, friends. I have come in answer to your questions."

"Yes, Lord," they reply as they rise to their feet.

The Lord invites them to sit in the golden chairs, and they do. You feel the Lord's powerful love for Moses and Adam. You can also feel that the Lord is very pleased with them. In fact, He is so pleased, He appears to be on the edge of rejoicing.

The Lord turns to address the multitude. He says warmly,

> "Brothers and sisters, there are treasures in all things. Inside each of you is infinite treasure. Before the beginning of your story, I hid treasures throughout many worlds, so that kings and queens could seek treasure and discover good things.
>
> "Your stories began in the foundation of all things. In my mind, I saw a great adventure that has no end. In my

substance, the adventure began. Out of myself, I formed many worlds with many beings. All of you are part of something greater than anyone can ever fully understand. Of the increase of glory and goodness, there will be no end."

You hear cheers of affirmation and joy throughout the multitude.

The Lord smiles and opens His arms. He says:

"In the journey of a life, there is uncertainty and risk. In the soil of risk, courage can spring forth. Out of courage, many unique and special glories blossom.

"Yet, in the soil of risk, there is also the potential for great disaster. I saw this potential clearly. So, before your story began, I prepared a plan to help you in disaster. I would enter your story. I would experience your griefs. I would work with you to restore what was broken.

"You all have been faithful servants and leaders. You have brought life to the creation I love. You have loved others in the face of their hostility. You have been courageous in your love. In the midst of suffering, your compassion has brought me tears of deep joy. I am forever grateful for your glorious work.

"Those of you who have come here from the earth have received a crown of life in my presence. My kingdom is in you, and you are in my kingdom, forever."

Applause erupts throughout the Inner Courts. Many people have tears in their eyes, including both Adam and Moses.

The Lord continues:

"Now, what about the separated souls? *Can a separated soul be given a place with us?* My question remains. I have asked you how you would feel if I offered a separated soul a body of life and a place with us. You have debated this question in the presence of love without arriving at an agreement. There is a great mystery yet to be revealed."

The Lord turns to Adam, saying,

"Adam's joy stretches across the heavens. He hears my joyful songs inside his heart. He finds my voice in many places. My voice enters every heart, every mind, and every place."

The Lord turns to Moses, saying,

> "Moses has spoken wisely. He discerns my voice inside his heart. Moses also has the keys to unlock every scroll he has ever seen."

Moses looks intently at the Lord. Then Moses leans forward and whispers something into the Lord's ear.

The Lord is smiling. He looks at Moses and asks, "May I?"

Moses nods.

The Lord speaks,

> "Moses has a question. He is asking me about the sheep and the goats. He wants to know if he is right about the timing of their separation. He wants to know if the chasm between the righteous and the wicked must remain forever, without end."

Moses slides to the edge of his seat. A hush falls upon the temple.

The Lord then turns to Adam. The Lord descends to one knee and bows His head low. He then rises and turns to Moses. Again, the Lord descends to one knee and bows His head low. The Lord rises and turns to the multitude. This time, the Lord descends to both knees and bows His head all the way to the ground. As His head touches the ground, gold and silver sparkles begin to shine among all the people.

You wonder why the Lord is bowing to His creatures. The inner voice quietly answers, "The Lord is here to serve, not to be served."

As you ponder what this means, the Lord lifts His head. His mouth opens, and the sound of thunder shakes the temple courts. From His mouth emerges a small scroll.

Still on His knees, the Lord takes the scroll from His mouth and offers it to Moses. Moses takes the scroll and reads it.

Adam asks, "What does it say, Moses?"

As Moses looks at the scroll, one of his eyebrows rises. Moses says, "The words on this scroll are the most profound words I have ever seen."

Adam replies, "Go on!"

Moses then turns his head sideways. "Actually, these are the least profound words I have ever seen."

Adam smiles. "Moses, are you teasing us?"

Moses grins. He lifts the scroll in the air.

"My friends, here is what the Lord's scroll says:

*'If the citizens of my perfect
kingdom can debate a
question, then I shall consider
that question debatable.'"*

Everyone stands silent. They are not sure what to make of the statement on the scroll. What is the Lord saying? Is He implying that there is not a right answer to His question? Everyone desires an interpretation of the words on the scroll.

The Lord stands tall. He smiles wide. The Lord turns to the multitude and asks,

*"How would you feel if I
offered one of the separated
souls a body of life and a place
with us?"*

CHAPTER SEVEN

Chamber of Torment

A T THIS TIME, the people of light feel the Lord's invitation to consider His question in a new way. Moses and Adam have already presented cases to determine whether restoration of a separated soul *could be consistent* with the nature of heaven and with God's character and revelation. But now the people in the Inner Courts feel the significance of the choice before them. The Lord has asked how the people of light would feel about the restoration of a separated soul. How *would* they feel? Would they be filled with delight, or would they feel violated? No one in the Inner Courts sees clearly how a separated soul could be restored. Even Adam, who has hope, does not see how it could be done. Yet, the people of light feel the thrill of the possibility emerging before them. Together the feelings and thoughts of the multitude collapse into the following message:

> "You are the Lord! We trust you. If you were to make an offer to a separated soul, we would be curious to see what would happen."

Upon receiving their message, the Lord's appearance changes to that of a grand Lion. The Lion roars, and you hear the invitation in your spirit,

> *"Come! Let us go before the great throne!"*

The Lions jumps off the platform and begins to trot toward the gigantic throne in the distance. The multitude in the temple courts follows the Lion. Adam and Moses walk side by side, talking quietly with one another as they walk. You listen to them as they speak to one another.

"What is the Lord about to do?" asks Moses.

Adam replies, with a shake of his head, "The Lord knows something we do not."

Moses hangs his head low in thought. Suddenly, Moses hears the voice of the Lord inside his heart. He raises his head, and his eyes widen.

"What is it?" Adam asks.

"We are about to face an... an impossible challenge," replies Moses hesitantly. His face has grown slightly pale.

"Moses, you are a man of the scrolls," Adam answers. "You know that nothing is impossible for the Lord." Adam's expression carries lightness and jest.

"Oh, Adam," Moses says in a labored tone, "What the Lord has revealed to me is enough to shake my faith."

Adam looks intently at Moses. His face is more serious now. "So, what did the Lord say? What could shake the faith of a man whose faith is as strong as a dozen pillars in the Inner Courts?"

Moses remains silent for some time. Then he says, "The Lord intends to make an offer to the darkest soul—the King of Hell himself—the one named Lucifer."

At the mention of the name of the cursed one, Adam's whole body recoils. "What?!" Adam exclaims. "Has the Lord forsaken all justice? How could the Lord decide to do such a thing? It makes no sense at all!" Adam's body is tense.

But after a moment, Adam's expression softens and his body returns to a state of rest. "Who am I to judge the Lord, Moses? I repent of my unbelief. The Lord has the deepest wisdom. In the Lord, there is no darkness or evil. There must be a good reason for this."

"Yes, Adam," Moses replies, as he stares off into the distance. "It has to do with the pillar of Agreements. The Lord has instructed me to say no more."

Adam and Moses walk in silence until they reach the majestic throne, where the light of the Eternal King is always shining.

You notice that the ground has changed from marble to something that looks like crystal. The atmosphere is growing heavy from the weight of the glory of the throne and of the authority it carries. You find it difficult to keep walking.

Someone beside you nudges your arm. You turn to her. She offers you a piece of fruit from Adam's tree. You gladly take the fruit and eat it. The fruit strengthens you, and your pace returns to full stride.

The Lion now stands before the throne. As the multitude gathers around, the Lion speaks:

> "Citizens of heaven, I will now bring before you a separated soul."

The Lion turns toward the throne and roars loudly. As He roars, a powerful wind blows. A vortex begins to open a portal, which appears at the front of the throne.

The quiet, inner voice reveals, "This portal is a portal to the realm of the separated souls, the realm of hell."

The portal continues to widen until it is wide enough for the Lion to fit. As soon as the portal becomes wide enough, the Lion jumps through.

A great shield appears in front of the portal. Upon the surface of the shield, there is an animated image displaying the Lion, large enough for all in the Inner Courts to see.

Everyone can see on the image that the Lion is falling through darkness. As He falls, flames of red and orange fire reach toward Him. It is not long before the Lion lands upon something that appears like molten lava.

The Lion shrieks in pain. Despite the pain, the Lion pushes forward. You begin to hear screams and loud cries coming from somewhere nearby. The Lion half walks, half swims through the molten lava. Faces of separated souls lunge out from the fire toward the Lion. They scream at the Lion:

"Shame on you! How could you leave us in this place of torment while you hide away in your luxurious palaces? How could you be so heartless? If you truly cared about us, you would take us out of this place. *Shame on you! Shame on you! Shame on you!"*

Every time you hear a shout of hatred, you see flames of fire leave their tongues. The flames burn the tormented souls as they scream. The flames also follow the path of their screams and rain upon the Lion's back.

The Lion presses on, wincing from the pain as each flame of fire licks His fur.

Ahead, there is a gigantic cliff. The Lion reaches the edge of the cliff and follows the molten lava off the side of it. He falls with the lava. As He falls, the air grows thicker and darker. The smoke and stench make it difficult for the Lion to breath. Yet, the Lion continues His descent.

The Lion falls and falls. Deeper and deeper into hell He goes. Eventually, you can tell that the Lion is nearing the bottom, because flames of fire have reached up to meet the Lion in the air. These flames are purple.

As the Lion continues to fall, blackness closes in on Him. If it were not for the radiant light within the Lion, He would not be visible at all. There is a loud thump. The Lion's paws hit the ground so hard that the ground cracks.

Hideous creatures lash out at the Lion as He steps across the black, dry, lifeless ground. The Lion passes by deformed lizards, venomous snakes, birds of ghastly appearance, and small imp-like creatures with torn flesh and exposed bones as He continues to walk.

One creature is the size of a rhinoceros, except with a wide, ugly head and large fangs. This creature jumps onto the Lion's back. He bites deep into the Lion's flesh, leaving large gouges. Claw marks cover one whole side of the Lion's body.

The horrid creatures that attack the Lion quickly retreat. None can remain in His presence for long.

The Lion now limps as He walks. Before Him are rows of dark beings. These beings hold spears in their hands and are outfitted with armor.

The beings heckle the Lion as He limps. "Where are you going, Lion? Have you lost your way?" Several of the dark beings kick the Lion as He passes.

The Lion makes no aggressive move toward any creature as He walks.

Now you can see something up ahead. It is a hideous sight. You see a huge throne, made of bones stained black with old blood and thorns as long as nails. The throne rests upon an elevated platform of black rock. Skulls surround the platform. A huge, bloodshot eyeball is embedded in the top of the throne. The eyeball constantly looks to and fro.

Before the throne, a dark beast is pacing. He has huge horns on his head and hooved back legs like a goat. His back is hunched. His skin is black and rough. His eyes are yellowish green, with horizontally-elongated pupils. His nose and mouth appear more like the snout of an animal than like the face of a man. He wears a black garment that looks something like a king's robe and cape. A spindly black crown sits upon his head. This is the King of Hell, also known as the Dark One.

The dark, beastly king appears surprised, frustrated, and angry all at once. He shrieks at the Lion, "Why are you here?" In a sudden panic, the beast looks down at himself. He straightens up so that he is standing as tall as he can. With his nose pointed high in the air, he says to the

Lion, "I know why you are here. You have come to acknowledge my glory!"

A blood curdling heckle emerges from the dark soldiers encircling the beast's throne.

The Lion says nothing. He simply stands before the beast as the dark creatures laugh.

"Well, then," the Dark One says, "now that you have finally come to your senses and realized my great power, I wonder how you will express your reverence for me. Will you bow down before me? Or will you kiss my feet?"

Laughter again erupts among the dark ones.

The Lion stands motionless.

When the Dark One sees that the Lion is not responding to his prods, hatred begins to boil in his veins. Dark, invisible flames—the hottest flames in all creation—burst out from the center of the evil throne and rain down upon the Lion's head. The Lion's mane is singed. Several of the Lion's whiskers are burned until they are mere smoldering stubs.

The dark beast turns and sits down on his throne. He laughs, "Is that fear I sense from you, oh King, who is self-exalted?"

The Lion remains completely still and silent.

Fury laces the words of the beast as he begins a monologue:

"Yes, you cowardly beast! That *is* fear I sense! You have always been afraid of me! You feared my independence since the day I grew up. You feared the day when my glory would outstrip yours. But there was nothing you could do to stop the inevitable!

"Shame on you, beast! Your appearance as a Lion is a farce. You are grasping for splendor that can never be yours! No one in your kingdom would love you if they knew what you really were!

"You are the most self-centered of all beings. You make your slaves pet you day and night. They pet you with blind praises. You keep all the glory for yourself!

"How do you reward those who pet you? You give them troubles and tribulations. And how do you reward those who *don't* pet you? You throw them away!

"Your kingdom is built upon burning coals of injustice, cruelty, and deception. Everyone in your kingdom suffers."

The beast then stands and yells, pointing at the Lion,

"You wicked beast! I despise you! You are eternally banned from my presence. You shall suffer outside my kingdom forever. Go back to your pitiful throne, you deceiver of all creatures! I condemn you to the outer darkness, where you will continue to suffer for your sins forever! May all creatures watch you get what you deserve! You shall suffer in your shame! Get away from me, you evildoer!"

The Dark One stomps his foot onto the ground, and the ground splinters into a million pieces. Flames burst through the cracks and burn all the creatures standing nearby.

With tenderness in His eyes, the Lion lifts His paw and says, "Come with me."

The beast stands in shock. He then shouts scornfully, "What?! You depraved beast! I cannot come with you! Have you forgotten that light and darkness cannot mix? I am the Light of the World. You are filthy. Rotten. Darkness is your name. Deception marks your tongue. You stupid, stupid beast. You cannot persuade me with your smooth lips. I will never relent my judgement. I will never have mercy on you! You will not trick me into following you into your place of torment.

You shall continue to suffer outside my presence forever. Go back to hell!"

With gentleness, the Lion again lifts His paw. "Come with me," the Lion says again. "I will go, but there is something I want you to see. I will put a shield around you to protect you from my kingdom. You will be safe."

Unrest permeates every being surrounding the throne. The Dark One paces quickly back and forth, muttering to himself. Several times, he quickly glances over his shoulder, as if afraid of something lurking in the darkness behind him. A frown overpowers his anxious expression, and he plunges himself down once more upon his throne.

The beast pounds his fist down upon the arm of the throne. He yells, "You arrogant, beast! What do you have to show me? Do you think you can impress me? Pride comes before a fall, beast!"

The Dark One pauses a moment. The beast lowers his voice as he speaks: "You are so ignorant and arrogant. How could you ever be taught right from wrong? But perhaps some of your followers are not as stupid as you. Perhaps some of them can still be freed from your deceit. Yes! I will save them. You stupid creature, take me to your kingdom! They will see my glory. And

I will expose to them your true nature. Then all the creatures in heaven and hell will know the truth!"

The Lion nods His head. When He does, a transparent, faintly glowing orb appears around the Dark One. A similar orb surrounds the Lion, and the two of them begin to travel back the way the Lion came. The orb shields the pain and torment being projected upon them as they move through the depths of hell. The Lion's wounds heal rapidly inside the orb as the two kings ascend from the depths. The orbs also accelerate their movement.

The kings of heaven and hell move up and up, out of the darkness, past the fire and molten lava, past the creatures shouting in agony, and toward the portal.

As they approach the portal to heaven, the Dark One shouts, "You won't trick me by leaving me behind. I will go first."

The Lion moves aside and allows the beast to enter first.

The multitude in heaven watches in near disbelief as the image on the shield displays the Dark One entering the portal that leads to heaven. The image on the shield fades. All eyes are on the portal. First comes the dark beast, still protected by his orb. Then comes the Lion.

There is a flash of light, and the portal seals behind them. The Lion and the Dark One stand in front of the great throne.

You hear gasps throughout the multitude.

The Lion addresses the multitude, "Citizens of my kingdom, this is the king of the darkest realm outside our presence."

At this announcement, murmuring erupts throughout the multitude.

The Dark One puffs up his chest and pushes his way in front of the Lion. As he does, the form of the Dark One changes. Now he appears as a radiant being. Long golden hair flows down to about mid-chest. His eyes are brilliant. Fluorescent streaks of light decorate the radiant glow surrounding his body. He is wearing a long white garment that is ornamented with gold. His gaze is mesmerizing.

"I am Lucifer, the One who shows everyone the path to understanding," says the radiant figure. His voice is as smooth as velvet, and his gestures as soft as a gentle stream. "This is my true form, which I now reveal to you. This Lion, who is more cunning than any beast, has tried to obscure my true nature from you. But I have come now to share with you the truth."

The Lion simply stands back and watches the being as he speaks. You wonder why the Lion does nothing. Many throughout the crowds talk quietly to one another concerning the unfolding events.

The glowing angelic creature continues:

"I have come to alleviate your heavy burdens and sorrows. In this Lion's kingdom, you are not free to do as you please. You are forced into servitude. You can never truly have what you want. This Lion whom you serve is full of twisted thorns that trick and trap you. Come with me, out of this deception. This place appears beautiful on the surface. But under the surface is darkness and deceit. These pillars do not contain the full truth.

"Come with me, and I will give you hidden knowledge that this Lion will never reveal to you. I will give you power that this Lion will never allow you to have. I will give you every experience you could ever desire. You will see that this Lion controls you by calling things evil that are not.

"Once your spirit is enlightened, you will see that you have always had the same power as this One whom you worship. His ploy will be exposed. Just as I have ascended, you will also ascend.

"Depart from this realm, free yourselves from the Lion's crushing control, and I will teach you the secrets of the universe. I will make you great. You shall be greater than the 'God' you now serve."

You notice that as the radiant angel speaks, small white snakes slither out of his mouth and wind around his body. The snakes coil around his arms, legs, neck, and head. At first, the angel pays no notice. But after some time, you can see that the strength by which the snakes coil around him is beginning to overpower him. He begins gasping for breath.

Nevertheless, the angelic being continues his proselytizing:

"Come with me, you who have slumbered in darkness, and I will teach you the ways of light. Do not hesitate, for today is the day of salvation. Follow me, and I will show you your true glory!"

Not one person in the Inner Courts is moved by the offer presented by the angelic being standing behind the shield. You wonder how this could be.

An inner voice says, "This is not the first time these people of light have encountered the voice of the deceiver. They have learned, through experience, to discern truth from lies. They are well aware of the devil's schemes."

When the radiant being sees that no one is accepting his offer, his anger surfaces violently.

The angel turns to the Lion and screams, "You depraved, immoral tyrant! You have brainwashed these subjects of yours beyond all rationality! You think you have power? Ha! You are an evil, merciless coward. Just go ahead and squeeze your fists tight. See how many of your precious creatures slip out of your hands!"

The atmosphere inside the angel's translucent sphere grows hotter and darker. The radiant appearance he had taken is slowly disintegrating. Fire flares up around the being as the intensity of his hatred increases. The fire smolders his flesh, and smoke fills the orb. The being has now returned to his beastly form. As the dark creature screams his accusations against the Lion, sharp objects thrust into his body. He shrieks in agony. Ages of bitterness begin to manifest upon the creature's body as horrid diseases and decay. Patches of skin that have burned or decayed with disease fall off the dark being's frame until his bones are visible. But as this happens, new skin appears, and the disease and burning spreads across his body again.

The Lion watches, motionless. He is waiting. You can sense it.

"What is He waiting for?" you wonder.

You can sense that the Lion is carrying a great weight of emotion and responsibility. There is great pain in His eyes.

Suddenly, the Lion roars loudly. From the throne, a great waterfall emerges. It pours down from the throne and rushes over the sphere where the Dark One resides. A cavern opens up in the ground under the sphere to swallow up the waterfall once it has passed over the sphere.

"The cleansing waters of heaven have been released," the Lion says quietly.

You wonder, "What is the meaning of this waterfall?"

A strong, yet peaceful, response comes to you within your spirit: "This waterfall comes from the tears the Lord has collected over the ages. These tears are from all those who have been injured by the Dark One, whose name is Lucifer. Lucifer must experience these tears. He has tried to run from them for ages and ages. But the time has now come for a great justice to be fulfilled."

Another question arises within you, "Is *this* how justice is fulfilled?"

You hear a voice inside you reply, *"Justice always serves souls."* Whether this voice is your own or the Lord's, you cannot tell.

"I do not understand," you say in your center. You await further clarification, but none comes. All you can do now is watch the events unfold before you.

The waterfall pours over the orb with great force. You can see behind the layers of rushing crystal water that the translucent globe is completely filled with dark smoke and thick blackness. The being inside the orb thrashes around, and you occasionally catch a glimpse of his form. The creature goes back and forth between shouting profanities to muttering to himself to yelling commands to chanting curses to writhing and shrieking. It is the most horrible thing you have ever witnessed.

You look toward the Lion. He stands at attention. You cannot tell what the Lion is thinking or what He is going to do next. He is as still as stone.

Above the Lion appears an image of a heart. The heart is beautiful, vibrant, and glowing. As you look into the heart, you notice a dark spot. Near the center of the heart, a bit toward the left side, there is a large dark splotch with an irregular shape. Within it, the flesh appears dead and decayed. Outside this dark spot, the heart is beating with joy and energy. Inside the dark spot, there is no life at all. You sense that the image displays the Lion's heart, and that it is only visible to those who are looking for it.

You hear a voice within you say, "As long as souls are separated from me, they are dead. If they are dead, part of Me is also dead. No height nor depth can separate Me from their torment."

The Dark One screams in rage, "Make it stop, you evil Lion! Stop this torture! STOP IT! Make it STOP!"

The Lion remains motionless.

The screaming continues, "STOP this, stop this NOW! I hate you with unceasing fury! I will NEVER acknowledge your glory. Never! Make it STOP, beast! You evil creature!" The Dark One cries out in pain, "MAKE IT STOP!"

The Lion's expression does not change.

You are immersed in the moment. It does not seem to have a beginning or end. The agony of the creature touches your center. The pain this creature has caused goes beyond measure, and yet, it is almost unbearable to witness his suffering. Perhaps your soul is not strong enough to bear such weighty things. You are glad that the Lion is nearby. Without His presence, you would not have the strength to stand.

The creature's screams and curses continue for a long time. The individual events meld together so that your experience of them feels like a murky mist.

You notice subtle streams of what looks like dark sediment mixing in with the crystal water as it passes over the dark orb where the beast resides. As you inspect the scene more closely, you are able to see what is happening with greater detail. As the water runs along the surface of the orb, small amounts of the darkness contained within the orb are sucked outward and swept away. The sheer force of the torrent pulls the darkness out of the orb, little by little, and puts in its place a substance of truth and brings healing and life. And yet, new darkness is constantly created within the orb by the creature's own choices. You cannot tell whether the level of darkness in the orb is increasing or decreasing at this point.

After a long while, the noise the Dark One is producing changes slightly in tone. Untempered force and aggression are now laced with intermittent whimpers of weakness. "I HATE you, I HATE you! This punishment is unbearable! Help me! I cannot endure this any longer!" Moans, pitiful cries, and long shrieks fill the sounds emerging from the orb. "Please! I will do anything! Release me now!" The beast's cries are now filled with bitterness, despair, and fear.

The Lion takes several steps forward until His orb is touching the orb of the Dark One. The Lion moves His head close to the edge and speaks:

> "The pain you are feeling now is the pain you inflicted upon others. Every fear, every heartbreak, every tear that you have ever caused is now pouring upon you. Lifetimes—eons—of pain are now pulsing through your soul. This pain shall be *everlasting*, because the destruction you have caused is *everlasting*. You must suffer *forever*."

The Lion then takes several paces back. He draws in a long breath and then projects four short grunts toward the dark orb.

Something has changed. You study the orb and see that the motion inside it is much faster than that outside. The water from the waterfall is also falling at a more rapid rate. As you watch, the waterfall and the orb continue to accelerate, as if they are transitioning to a different timeline. The motion increases, faster and faster. Now the motion has accelerated to such a speed that time appears to stand still. The waterfall now looks like a motionless cylinder. The orb is nothing more than a dark cloudy ball. The motions and sounds of the creature inside are now so fast that they are indiscernible to you.

Still, you can pick up various thought forms and penetrating arrows of emotion as you focus on the sphere. Horror. Rage. Pain. Excruciating pain. You feel the overwhelming chorus of thoughts, screams, yells, whimpers, and pleas. The creature weeps with no hope of relief.

Everyone before the throne witnesses the dramatic display of torment. Adam and Moses stand silent. Moses has tears rolling down his cheeks.

Many thoughts and questions are splintering throughout the multitude:

"Why is the Lion showing us this suffering?"

"Did He want to bring a separated soul before us to teach us the horrors of evil?"

"Did the Lord trick the Dark
One into coming here so that
his torture would be displayed
before the entire kingdom?"

"Are we seeing the true nature
of justice?"

You hear a being to your left ask, "Who is the Lion?"

Another being on your right says, "Is the Lion truly as wise and loving and good as we have been led to believe?"

You feel a scent of fear sweeping across the beings near you.

Inside your own heart, you hear a quiet, familiar voice. *"Truth takes time,"* the voice echoes within you.

Everyone looks to the Lion. The Lion is motionless and speechless. He simply faces the orb and watches.

Adam looks to Moses. He asks, "Moses, has the Lord revealed anything to you about the nature of this judgement?"

Moses replies in a cracked voice, "This creature is bound by the Agreement of Souls. I cannot say anything more."

You sense that everyone is acutely aware of the intense suffering the dark soul is experiencing. When you ponder the situation, the suffering seems impossible to fathom. How many ages has the Dark One experienced within the orb? What is the intensity of his suffering? What would it be like to suffer *forever*? Even as you ponder these questions, you know the torment continues.

Everyone is wondering what to do.

CHAPTER EIGHT

Eve Speaks

I
N THE MIDST of silence, you hear someone shuffling through the multitude, from near where Adam and Moses are standing. You catch a glimpse of the long, wavy brown hair before you identify who the person is. It is a woman. She reaches a place near the front, next to Adam and Moses, beside where the angelic creature and the Lion stand. As she turns around, you recognize her face. It is Eve, the mother of all humans.

Eve looks at Adam. Adam looks back at Eve with admiration and approval. You can tell that these two have a special connection, as well as high respect for one another.

"The Lord has impressed a message upon me," Eve says to Adam quietly.

"Do not hesitate to share your wisdom with us," Adam replies. "You see truths by the light of your experience that we do not yet see."

Eve looks back toward the Lion and discovers that the Lion is already looking toward her. From the Lion's heart emerges a thick cloud of light that wisps through the air and wraps itself around Eve. The light forms into an ornate garment that accentuates Eve's beauty, strength, virtue, and wisdom. The garment, though taking the appearance of delicate queenly apparel, is as strong as the armor of light that had clothed Moses and Adam as they prepared to address the multitude in the Inner Courts.

You hear a quiet voice within you say, "Invite Eve to speak."

You send your approval and encouragement to Eve. Sparkling, vibrant energy flows from your center toward her. All the people before the great throne invite Eve to speak. Energy flows to Eve from the multitude so that she is shining brilliantly. You can see that she is greatly encouraged and strengthened by the positive intentions directed toward her from every being.

Eve then faces the multitude and begins to speak:

> "Children of heaven, a deeply troubled soul—this king of darkness—is suffering in our midst. I ask you, how can suffering exist in the realm of heaven? For the sake of peace, this horror must be removed from our sight.
>
> "But, I tell you the truth, even if we removed this horror from our sight, there would *still* be suffering in our midst."

Eve looks back at the Lion. Then she faces the multitude and gestures back toward where the Lion stands. She continues:

> "Our Lord suffers, like a mother who sees her child suffering. Does a mother only suffer when her child suffers innocently? What if the child's suffering is self-inflicted? What if the child's suffering is deserved from the child's foolish actions? Does the mother no longer suffer with her child?
>
> "I tell you, people of light, a mother suffers when her child suffers. Even if the child runs away from the mother's love and scorns her affection, the mother can

never lose her love for her child. With love comes empathy. With empathy comes a vulnerable heart. I ask you, could a mother ever be fully happy while she knows her child is suffering?"

Passion and conviction grow inside Eve like a fire. You feel the energy of her words.

Eve looks back at the orb. Then she looks back at the Lion. The Lion's eyes are fixed on the spherical chamber where the dark beast is suffering.

Eve stands upright and turns toward the multitude. She addresses the people with boldness:

"Sons and daughters of the Eternal King, hear what I have to say. The dark soul in our midst faces a judgment we cannot fathom.

"We suffer by the sight of this beast's suffering. But would our suffering end if this beast were no longer in our sight? It would not. We would still suffer, knowing that this beast is suffering somewhere *separated* from our presence. Even if the suffering of this beast were blocked from our sight—and removed from our memory—that would still not eliminate all suffering in heaven.

"Remember, the Lord also suffers as the beast suffers. Can the Lord, the Ruler of Heaven and Earth, choose not to see or even remember the suffering of this dark soul? It is written, 'If I ascend to the heavens, you are there; if I make my bed in the depths, you are there.' Where could we possibly send a soul to escape the Lord's sight? I tell you, the suffering of even one soul, even the darkest of souls, will be felt by the Lord.

"Children of the Most High, I present to you a mystery: how can heaven be fully *heaven* while there remains the pain of seeing someone in hell?"

Eve pauses. You feel the inner conflict experienced in the hearts of the people of light gathered before the Lord's throne. You feel the weight of the dilemma as well. The thought crosses your mind, "Perhaps the waterfall of tears will run its course. Perhaps the water will run dry. Then, maybe, the beast's suffering will end and the demands of justice will be met."

The quiet inner voice replies, "What if the waterfall can never end? What if the tears are multiplied as time goes on? What if the demands of justice can never be met?"

You feel deep pain emerge in your heart. The pain is unrelenting. It is almost unbearable. You look toward the Lion and see that He is looking toward you. His eyes are piercing. You understand, by the gaze of the Lion's eyes, that the pain you are experiencing is just a taste of His pain. You cannot imagine holding this pain inside you for any longer. Immediately, the pain subsides, and you feel deep comfort from the Lion's loving expression.

You ask the Lion, with the inner voice of your heart, "Is the suffering you feel truly so great? How can you suffer so intensely and yet give such powerful love to all of us here?"

The quiet whisper of the Lord replies, "My heart is large enough for all the cosmos to fit inside." The Lion's gaze then returns to the dark orb and the suffering beast.

Your attention returns to Eve. You can see that she is conflicted. Yet, her conviction remains. Something inside of you wonders, "Is there some way—*any* way—this suffering can end?"

The emotions of the multitude run high. Everyone feels the significance of the suffering taking place, especially the suffering of the Lord.

Many have tears in their eyes as they experience the reality of the suffering. There is a desire growing within the multitude—the desire for the suffering to end.

The desire for the suffering in heaven to end builds. As it builds in size and power, something strange happens. The desire of the multitude takes a mysterious form. The intense emotions collect into a single point, just as matter and energy collect into the singularity of a black hole.

Suddenly, a violent shock wave erupts from the singularity. The translucent ripple of energy spreads almost instantly through the atmosphere. The wave pulses through the translucent shield that separates the multitude from the fallen angel's orb. The water from the waterfall evaporates. The orb shatters. Shards of light sprinkle across the multitudes.

Everyone watches in shock.

Lucifer is no longer in his cage of torment. The beast is now free.

CHAPTER NINE
The Separated Soul Speaks

THE BEAST FALLS to the ground. He is curled up tightly.

No one says a word. You wonder what will happen next.

The Lion walks close to the pitiful creature who is rolled up in a ball on the ground. Instead of towering over the creature, the Lion kneels on the ground beside him. Tears stream from the Lion's glossy eyes, down his cheeks, and onto His mane. Emotions of love pour out of the Lion's chest in the form of gentle waves. The waves flow from the Lion's chest to the dark creature beside him.

On top of the waves, you notice scrolls. "What are these scrolls?" you ask with your inner voice.

Knowledge comes to you. "These scrolls are messages of wisdom and love from the Lord," the inner voice explains.

The scrolls drift over the waves of love. They land upon the creature's back. As the scrolls touch the beast, they dissolve into him, absorbing into his core. You see tears rolling down the beast's face.

The multitude joins the Lion in expressing love toward the beast. Waves of love roll out of every being. The love emanating from each being has a unique pattern, texture, color, and appearance.

All the waves of love join the Lion's waves of love. The combination produces a spectacular display of dancing energy. The colorful waves of love wash over the beast, carrying with them positive affirmation, encouragement, strength, and joy.

The waves of love fall upon the beast for what seems like ages and ages.

Slowly, the beast uncurls. The beast begins to stand. As he rises to his feet, everyone continues to pour out loving affirmation toward him. The Lion also stands, shadowing the motion of the creature beside Him.

You wonder what it must be like to be that creature. You cannot comprehend the history of evil and of the hardening of his heart, or of the ages of suffering that followed. You wonder what was written on the scrolls that moved this creature to tears. You also wonder what it was like for this creature to be washed over with waves of love after dwelling in evil for so long. Could a creature like this actually receive such love?

As the creature lifts himself up, tears continue to stream down his face. Once he is standing on two feet, he immediately begins to weep. The emotion of the weeping is pure and humble. It is a weeping of sincere sorrow, along with deep pain, but it is also a weeping of relief and surprise.

The emotion of the creature's weeping touches all those present, and everyone weeps with the creature who is now free. The Lion also weeps.

After a long time, Moses steps closer to the creature. Tears are falling from Moses' eyes. With tenderness, Moses bends down on one knee and asks the creature, "Tell us, why are you weeping?"

The creature looks out across the multitude. Everyone sends their feelings of love and approval to the creature standing before them. There is not one feeling of judgement, accusation, or doubt in their midst. All are curious to listen to whatever the creature has in his heart to say.

"My tears... come from a feeling... I can hardly... describe," the creature says between deep heaves. As he speaks, there is something about his physical appearance that seems to change.

You feel the waves of approval rushing past you toward the creature. The feeling is that of safety and peace. You hear the thoughts of many: "It's okay. We're here with you. You're okay."

The creature takes in a deep breath. He lets out a sigh as he looks out across the multitude. He then begins to speak, with tears still in his eyes:

> "Citizens of heaven, kings and queens,
> I am ruined in your presence. Your light
> is glorious. Your love is pure."

The creature's voice cracks, as he holds back his tears. He continues:

> "My experience and perspective have
> transformed in ways that are difficult to

explain. I now understand, from the Lord's light, that my experience in the orb moved much faster than yours... thousands of times faster... millions of times faster. Because of this, I may have difficulty communicating to you what has happened to me. Yet, I will try."

The creature pauses, looking down. Again, he is choking back tears. He continues:

"My experience of torment endured for a time I cannot measure. During this time, I began to comprehend a meaning that I had not previously understood. Every painful experience was a syllable in a sentence, which conveyed to my center a deeper insight into the meaning of what I had done."

There is certainly something different about the creature's appearance now. His face has softened. His body is less rigid. His robes are less sinister. His facial features seem to be much more angelic in likeness now. His robes are a shimmering navy blue. It even looks as though his hind legs may have transformed. The creature is now standing straighter and taller than before.

The creature glances toward Moses as he continues. The creature explains:

"My experience of precise pains gave precise meanings to ancient thoughts. I always knew that many of the evils I inflicted on others were bad. But there is a meaning I could not know without experience. The deepest experience unlocks the deepest meaning. Experience fills up meaning with a significance that cannot be described with mere words. In my experience of intense torment, my heart drank in an intense understanding of the badness of the pain I had inflicted on others."

The creature looks down and again begins to weep. Moses lays a reassuring hand on the creature's shoulder.

The creature gathers himself and continues:

"When the torment began, I was exploding with rage. I felt the power I once had slip away from me. I could not give a command or speak a word or chant a spell to change my torment. All I could think was, 'This is not fair! This is not right! This should not be happening to me!' As my suffering increased, my rage flared with unquenchable fury and hatred.

"At first, I could not admit to myself the level of darkness within myself, though I could always feel it.

"I became angry at all those who stole glory, power, recognition, pleasure, and significance away from me. As I dwelt upon the injustice of this thievery, my hatred boiled.

"Soon the pain became so intense that all I could think about was myself. I began to focus on the things that I knew were lacking within me. The pain was so pointed I could not resist its pressure to look inward. I saw the lack within myself. My internal lack caused me extreme anger. The more I reflected upon my lack, the angrier I became at myself and at the One who created me.

"Yet after ages of torment, I could no longer continue to fuel my intense anger. The pressure of my suffering caused my anger to collapse into shame. The shame was overwhelming. I cannot fully describe to you the intensity of the shame I felt.

"I had known from the beginning, deep down, that my suffering was my own doing. I ran from this knowledge. I hated this knowledge. But with no end of torment in sight, my strength to run eventually failed. I finally broke. I could no longer avoid facing the knowledge of what I had done.

"When I stopped running, the weight of my shame fell upon me. The shame was so heavy upon me that I could not breathe. I had no will to live. Yet, I could not die.

"My shame gave birth to deep despair. My pride was gone. My anger was gone. All that remained was the suffering of shame and despair. There was nothing else I could do. There was no hope. I believed I could never escape."

The creature looks back at the Lion. Upon seeing the Lion, the creature begins to weep once more. The Lion breathes a sparkling blue mist from His mouth onto the creature. The mist strengthens and encourages the creature so that he can regain his composure.

The creature's eyes are rounder now, and his face is more refined. He looks over the multitude with a penetrating gaze that draws out the depths of each soul. He speaks once more:

"I will not lie to you, creatures of goodness. I did not have the power in my heart to repent of my evil ways. I was crushed under the weight of my shame and torment, and my soul did not have the strength or the will to look beyond itself.

"But suddenly, without expectation or warning, something happened to me. In the midst of my hopeless, shriveled, tormented existence, there was a brilliant, majestic sound. It was the sound of the desire of your hearts. This sound shattered my chamber of torment and awakened hope within my soul. Your *hope* set me free!

"Yet, I was still paralyzed on the inside. Ages and ages of trauma and isolation depleted me of all power. I could not move.

"Then, something surprising and glorious happened. I felt your great approval washing over me. This feeling of authentic approval was like a distant memory. As your love began to cover me,

I did not feel worthy to receive it. Yet, in my empty state, I was now desperate to drink it.

"The shame within me burned like a raging fire with each passing wave of love. How could I accept such love? I felt your love would certainly destroy me. Everything within me wanted to curl up into nothingness and hide.

"Yet, the gentle waves of love continued washing me, beckoning me out from the darkness. Though I tried to hide, the love was relentless. Waves of great love continued flowing from the great Lion, and from all of you.

"'How could such souls as these love me?' I wondered. 'I have hurt these souls with the vilest of evils and hatred. How could they extend to me love so pure?'

"In the midst of the continuous waves of love, the Lion sent me messages of wisdom written on many scrolls. The messages came alive in me. The history of all my experiences unlocked the meaning of these messages. They imparted to me a new interpretation of reality that allowed me to see many truths.

"The scrolls painted a picture of history. In this picture, I saw the presence of the Lord's love for me in every moment and situation. I received an understanding of the great pains I caused the Lord, along with the Lord's enduring grace and mercy.

"I learned that every pain I suffered, the Lord also suffered with me. The Lord revealed to me that His heart could not be separated from my pain, because of how much He loves me.

"Then, as I continued to interpret the scrolls, I discovered a great truth I had never before understood. It is a truth about me. The Lion revealed to me who I really am."

Upon sharing these words, the creature weeps again. All the people in heaven are fully present in the experience of this moment. The experience is real and raw.

Adam steps up. He walks between the creature and the multitude. Adam holds up his hands protectively, saying,

"Listen, oh heavenly beings! What the Lord has spoken to this creature is personal. The Lord has revealed hidden things, secret things, into every heart. These hidden truths are enclosed within unique chords of love. It is not our place to know what the Lord has spoken to the one standing before us. Some things are too personal and intimate for everyone to know. Some revelations belong only to the one to whom they are revealed."

Adam places his hand on the creature's shoulder and blesses him. The multitude again sends their approval and love toward the creature, whose weeping is now starting to subside.

Adam and Moses step back and once more give the creature center stage. You notice that the creature's face is now slender and smooth. His hair is no longer ragged and rough, but now falls gently around his face.

The creature again speaks:

"What I have learned has shaken me. I cannot share everything the Lord has spoken to me, for only I have the precise experiences to unlock the precise meaning of His revelation to me. No mere words can express the fullness of the Lord's revelation. But I can tell you a story to help you understand.

"Ages ago, I was placed in charge of overseeing these temple courts. The Lord gave me great power, beauty, talent, and glory. Yet, the Lord hid my glory many times in front of many creatures.

"The Lord invited me to elevate the glory of others. The Lord also demonstrated what it looks like to elevate the glory of others. At first, I felt sad when the Lord did not display my glory. Then, I became bitter. Whenever another creature's glory was set up on display, jealousy ravaged my heart.

"Jealousy grew inside of me. In my jealousy, my mind became darker. Truths twisted into new forms. I began to see the Lord in a different light. To me, the God of creation was not a God of power but of weakness, not a God of wisdom but of ignorance, and not a God of justice but of injustice. I believed I knew better how to rule. I wanted things to be different. I wanted God's throne.

"My jealousy turned to anger, and my anger turned to hatred. In my hatred, I could no longer perceive the wisdom of the Lord.

"I didn't understand that the Lord hides the greatest treasures for kings and queens to search out and discover. I didn't realize that the Lord was hiding my glory for a great discovery. The Lord had put me in charge of many things, but I did not understand why the Lord restricted me from displaying my greatest capacities.

"I felt that God did not have my best interest in mind. I believed God was deceiving me, and that He wanted all the glory for Himself. I began to believe that the God of the universe was an evil being.

"So I recruited beings to establish a new kingdom. I imagined that my kingdom was the true kingdom of light, truth, and wisdom. I violently opposed God and all of His ways. All of these events occurred before the human story began.

"When the Lord brought humans onto the earth, I was frustrated. These tiny, insignificant beings could not compare to my glory and splendor. Yet, the Lord elevated them beyond what they deserved. I wanted to show them the truth about my glory. I wanted to rule them—to rule *you*. I also wanted to hurt God for hurting me.

"As I sought to rule humans, my kingdom grew in power. I tried to make my glory known to the nations of the earth. I tried to make beings above the earth, on the earth, and under the earth see my glory.

"But I saw, as my kingdom grew, that my kingdom was not secure. Rebellion was lurking in every corner. Those who became close to me were the likeliest to betray me. The only way I could maintain my power was to force those under my power to remain obedient to me and my ways.

"To maintain my control, I created punishments for those who did not meet my expectations. If they failed, they would suffer. If they succeeded, I would give them power, fame, wealth, and pleasure. If any creature began to waiver in their affections, I would instruct my generals, kings, and underlings to heap accusation, shame, and punishment upon that creature until they repented and conformed to my ways.

"I used threats, violence, manipulation, lies, and entrapment to force free beings to follow me.

"For a time, my kingdom grew without fetter. I was pleased with the progress I was making. God's kingdom was weak in comparison. I could easily overthrow it. At least, that is what I thought.

"However, as time progressed, I began to discover strange twists in response to my tactics. In the development of the human story on Earth, I constantly challenged God's rule. Yet the citizens of God's kingdom would not easily change their allegiance. I was angry that anyone would remain loyal to a God who allowed them to be beaten down and destroyed.

"I offered rewards for loyalty in my kingdom, yet my subjects would prove fickle. I could not understand why my kingdom kept slipping through my fingers. Your recalcitrance fueled my anger.

"I saw only one way to sustain my kingdom. I had to destroy every alternative to my kingdom. I had to destroy everyone who refused to submit to my rule.

"Now that I stand here before you, I understand why the Lord limited my rule. It was for my own benefit. He wanted me to learn the ways of His kingdom. I did not see the wisdom of His invitation. Instead, I scoffed at His ways and created my own.

"My scoffing paved a path for my kingdom—which is the kingdom of hell.

"Over all this time, I believed a lie, which formed in the soil of my jealousy. I thought that the Lord wanted to keep my deepest desires from me. I didn't understand that the Lord *wanted me to rule*. I didn't understand that the Lord wanted everyone to see my glory. I didn't understand that the Lord was preparing every new creature to discover my greatness. I didn't understand that the Lord wanted me to experience the deepest desires of my heart, and that nothing good was forbidden from me. My own jealousy, pride, and hatred blocked my sight of this wisdom. I didn't even look for this truth.

"I now understand that even my torment served me. The ages of torment caused me to experience the full badness of the foundations of the kingdom I had built. If the Lord had allowed me to run free for eternity, I would have continued to call evil good and good evil. I would have never seen or experienced the truth.

"Once you shattered my prison of shame, I experienced love in a way I was never able to before. I experienced love in the midst of all that I had done wrong. I experienced love from the very ones I hurt the most.

"In my experience of your love, I encountered a great truth previously hidden from my sight. I learned that the Lord's love for me never diminished, despite all that I had done. The Lord has never lost sight of the glory He designed me to carry. God still sees me as glorious. When this truth penetrated my heart, my shame rolled away. That is when I began to weep.

"You asked me why I was weeping. My weeping streams from an ocean of emotions I cannot express. Gratitude. Sorrow. A depth of understanding. Hope. Joy."

The creature now has a heavenly appearance. Bowing low to the ground, the creature addresses the multitude with great humility and reverence:

> "My words cannot make up for the torments I have caused. I ruled among you deceptively, often discreetly. I ruled inside dark corners of your governments, organizations, and family structures. I taught many of your leaders to control you with fear and shame.
>
> "Many tribes of hatred formed around my ideals. My tribes carried different flags, but on every flag you could find three words without fail: ACCUSATION, CONTROL, SHAME. These flags came into every nation, every tribe, and every religious sect. I loved those who loved me, and I shamed those who opposed me.
>
> "I tried to rule you so you could feel my greatness. I tried to rule you so I could feel my own greatness."

The creature turns to Eve:

> "Eve, daughter of the Ever-Living God, you were my nemesis. I was jealous of you. I didn't understand why the Lord

turned all attention to your kind, and I hated that he endowed you with such wisdom and beauty. I wanted what you had. I wanted to take your beauty and high position for myself. That is why I targeted you.

"Then, throughout the ages, I hurled insults and accusations against you and your offspring. My violence against you grew in the soil of my greatest fear—that I was not truly valued.

"I took advantage of you and your kind and pulled you into my rebellion. Words cannot convey my sorrow. I admit the evil of my ways."

Tears pour down the creature's cheeks as he cries out:

"I express to you my deep remorse, dear citizens of heaven! I do not deserve to be with you. I do not deserve your love. Yet, your love frees me. Without your love, I would still be suffering without hope. In your love, my fear flees. What would have become of me without you? I am humbled before you now. I stand before you, at your mercy."

The creature turns to the Lion. "Here I am in your midst, free from torment. What will you do with me now?"

All await the Lion's response.

The Lion steps forward so that He is standing beside the angelic being. The Lion looks across the sea of faces gazing back at Him.

The Lord asks, in a gentle voice,

> "Children of light, you have witnessed the testimony of this soul who was separated from us for ages and ages. What do you say I should do with this creature?"

As you gaze upon the Lion's expression, you notice that His appearance begins to change. The Lion transforms into a small Lamb.

The Lamb is innocent and powerless. The Lamb bleats, like a baby crying for its mother. The Lamb has a look of hope in its eyes.

Hearts are heavy with compassion and sorrow. Everyone carries a grain of the pain the Dark One experienced for so long.

Many people are also feeling another source of sorrow: the sorrow of separation. The Dark One was not the only one who suffered separation. *Everyone* suffered loss. When one soul is separate, all souls suffer the loss of the unique and special relationship with that soul.

Among the multitude, there is no disagreement. Everyone replies in unison:

> "May you be forgiven of all your sins. May you be washed clean, as white as snow."

The Lamb transforms into a Lion once more. He speaks gentle words to the creature: "May you be washed clean, as white as snow."

At the Lion's words, a brilliant light erupts from the creature with an array of colorful rainbows. Once the brilliant flash subsides, you can see that the creature has fully transfigured into a glorious angel. He is enrobed with white and gold, and his features carry magnificence and splendor. He is the most beautiful being you have ever seen.

The Lion faces the angelic being squarely and says,

> "You, my angel, are a great light. Today, your name is restored. Your name shall no longer carry shame. Instead, your name will be renowned as a glorious, blessed name. From this day forward, you

shall be called 'Lucifer' by all, for all shall know you as the Lord's light bearer."

Great sounds of cheering and crying fill the temple. The multitude carries many emotions in many forms. Some are singing. Some are crying. Some are silent. All are filled with joy.

Yet, underneath all these emotions, there still remains a current of curiosity. You ponder the scene before you. You can hardly believe your eyes. Is it really true? The greatest of all evils has come to an end? The most wicked being in history is now shining with magnificent glory?

"How has this happened?" you wonder.

You hear the inner voice say, "A great mystery is yet to be revealed."

CHAPTER TEN
Seven Secrets Revealed

THE LION TURNS toward the large throne behind Him. The Lion roars with a loud and thunderous sound. The ground shakes. Up from the ground, in front of the throne, billows dark smoke. As the shaking stops, clouds of smoke before the throne roll away. As the smoke clears, you see a large golden door.

The golden door is bound with chains. Each chain has a lock. You count seven chains with seven locks hugging the door tightly.

The Lion turns again to face the crowds. He addresses the people, saying,

"Royal creatures, it is time to reveal seven secrets of heaven. These secrets are ancient truths. Many of you have known some of these truths in part because of the path of experiences your soul has traversed. Your experiences unlock your insights. Today, in the midst of new experiences, a fuller meaning can be revealed to all who are gathered here.

"You have gathered here today to discover how a separated soul could be restored to us. You see before your eyes that a separated soul is now with us. But how has this happened? Seven keys will unlock this great mystery. You are now ready to understand how hell can be transformed into heaven."

The Lion walks to the door. He rubs his nose on the seven locks. The Lion continues to speak in a gentle, yet powerful, voice:

"Creatures of heaven, the seven secrets I am about to reveal to you will serve as seven keys to unlock these seven locks. Together, these seven keys will unlock this golden door."

Adam steps forward and inquires of the Lion, "But Lord, what is this golden door, and where does it lead?"

The Lion turns to Adam, and with a twinkle in His eye, He replies, "The insights you are about to encounter will prepare you to interpret the meaning of this door and to embark on the pathway of purposes awaiting you on the other side of it."

The Lion looks back toward the golden door. The first lock and chain begin to glow with a radiant light. Golden letters appear above the door, saying,

"GOD'S GREATEST FEAR."

"Citizens of my kingdom, listen to what I have to say," calls the Lion. He stands before the multitude with dignity and courage. You can sense that in His courage, the heart of the Lion is also vulnerable.

The Lion continues, "The first insight we will unlock together is an insight into the greatest fear of the Lord. My greatest fear is the fear of being separated from those I love—forever."

The Lion turns to Lucifer and speaks:

"This first insight is about you, my beloved angel. Lucifer, you have a great power to affect my emotions. I traveled through the caverns of darkness to reach you. But when I stood in your presence, you felt something inside of me. Do you remember what you felt? You said you sensed *fear* in me. You were right, Lucifer. I was afraid.

"You, my dear angel, didn't understand my fear or your power. You had the power to make me tremble. I trembled at the thought of losing you.

"I felt pain when you cast me out from your presence. My love for you never runs dry. Even if you cast me away, my desire for your flourishing never ceases.

"When you fell into the pit of darkness, I was grieved by the thought that you would continue to walk in your shame, isolation, fear, and brokenness. I wanted you to experience your full greatness, and to discover the secret treasures I hid away for you to find. I tell you the truth: there are still many more treasures hidden away for you that no eye has seen."

The Lion faces the multitude once again. He continues in a gentle voice:

"Citizens of heaven, I do not delight in the destruction of the wicked. While a soul is separated from me, my joy is not complete. I see all things in heaven and in hell. When I see heaven, I am delighted. But as long as there is hell, my feelings are mixed with grief.

"All beings are connected. Every being affects me. The separation of a soul causes me great sorrow, even while I am with you in heaven. As long as there is hell, heaven is not complete.

"My love for Lucifer was so great that I would do anything to restore him to wholeness. If I could suffer the torments of hell a million times over in his place, I would do it. But no suffering on my part could by itself turn his heart.

"I saw only one path leading to hope. On this path, the Dark One would experience the full consequences of his internal darkness in our presence. Although I knew the pain would be intense, it is better to suffer in heaven, with hope, than to suffer in hell, with no hope. I saw that in his suffering, there was a chance we could reach his heart. This path of pain was the only way to help the dark creature discover sincere sorrow and understanding.

"My greatest fear was that my love would remain hidden and that my dear angel would continue to suffer."

The golden words above the door form into the shape of a key.

The Lion says,

"This key is the first insight: *the Lord's greatest fear is of losing those He loves forever.*"

The key floats into the first lock on the door. "Open!" says the Lion. The key turns, the lock opens, and the first chain falls to the ground. Six locks remain.

All watch as the Lion again moves close to the door. As the Lion steps, He begins to glow brightly. Within the glow, you see the hints of human feet instead of Lion's paws. The glow subsides, and you see that the Lion has once again transformed into a glorious man. The man's features are soft, and his body gives off a gentle light.

The man stands before the door, and the second lock and chain glow. The man touches the second lock with one hand. The golden letters above the door form a new message:

"YOUR GREAT POWER."

The Lord looks toward the multitude and speaks:

"I will now reveal to you the second insight. This insight is about forgiveness.

"As you have known for many ages, forgiveness heals relationships. When anyone harms another being, the relationship between the beings is injured. This injury can heal, but the healing of all relationships must come through the door of forgiveness. Without forgiveness, an injury remains."

"You also know that forgiveness is not cheap. When you forgive someone, you offer a gift that costs you something.

"Citizens of heaven, you have a great power over darkness. You have power to transform darkness into light. You used your power to help turn even the darkest soul to its greatest light.

"When I brought Lucifer, who was the Dark One, into heaven, I protected him inside an orb. The orb served to shield the

Dark One from the scorching fire of righteousness he would have otherwise experienced in the Inner Courts of heaven. The orb provided a barrier between the kingdoms of hell and heaven. The barrier protected all of us from a violent reaction between two realms.

"The orb also served another purpose. Inside the orb, the beast could not escape the depravity of his spiritual condition. The orb provided a mirror from which the beast could not hide.

"I stood by and watched as the Dark One experienced his judgement. I hated to see his suffering. But his suffering was a means to reach his heart.

"I will now reveal to you a new insight. I will tell you why I could not fully heal Lucifer without your help.

"Many of you were wondering why I continued to let Lucifer suffer in our presence. You wondered why I did not set him free from his chamber of torment. The reason I could not set him free was that his heart was not changed. And his heart could not change unless he experienced your love for him. He needed to experience love and forgiveness from those he hurt. When you desired to set him free, he experienced a delicate sweetness of personal, vulnerable, brave, gracious love that he had never before tasted.

"Listen, kings and queens of heaven. I tell you a great truth. The Nobles were right: righteousness and justice prevented me from allowing a separated soul to have a place with us. By my righteousness and justice, I could not allow a separated soul to come into your presence without your consent."

"My precious children, you have the authority to refuse the presence of those who have caused you harm. The beast harmed you. You did not have to accept him. I could not force reconciliation. Only *you* had the power and authority over your response. Only *you* could decide whether you would forgive the beast for all the harms he committed against you.

"Each soul has the power and authority to seek to heal relationships, or to estrange relationships. I could not heal Lucifer's relationship with you unless you formed the desire to pursue healing of that relationship through the doorway of forgiveness.

"Understand this: my forgiveness for the beast was always there to be discovered. If he had sought my forgiveness, he would have found it. All who seek my treasures will find them.

"But my forgiveness was not enough to heal every relational tie that had been damaged. He needed your forgiveness, too. Your forgiveness was a key to unlock his repentance. As long as his relationship with you was injured, he could not be restored to you. Each of you had to decide to cancel his debt *to you* by your own will. Otherwise, he would not be able to enjoy relationship with you.

"As the beast suffered, you each became aware of the ways the beast had harmed you. You saw these harms with clarity, and you gained the power to forgive the beast.

"You understood the high price of forgiveness, and you chose to pay the price. You desired to let the beast go free from his chamber of torment. You sought to heal your relationship with the beast.

"Your act of love required vulnerability. You did not yet know if the beast would enter through the door of forgiveness in pursuit of healing. He could have rejected you. Yet, your offer of forgiveness provided an essential piece of Lucifer's restoration, without which such restoration would have been impossible.

"There is a great truth about your power, which was hidden until you used your power to set the Dark One free. Your expression of forgiveness awaked life inside his heart so that he could repent. If you had not forgiven him, perhaps no amount of suffering would have changed his heart."

The golden words above the golden door form into a key and float downward into the glorious man's hand. The man holds the key up into the air and announces,

"This key is the second insight: *you have the power to transform hell by the power of forgiveness.*"

Turning toward the door, the man extends the key outward and inserts it into the second lock. He steps back and commands, "Open." The lock opens, and the second chain falls to the ground. Five locks remain.

Another lock and chain glow like molten iron. This time, the Lord does not step forward to touch the lock. Rather, the Lord looks beyond the door to where Moses is standing.

"Moses," says the glorious man, "you carry within you a new revelation from the Spirit of the Lord. Share with us what you have learned, my son."

Moses elegantly gaits toward the golden door. The Lord gestures for Moses to stand beside the glowing lock and chain. Moses reaches out and touches the lock with one hand. The golden letters above the door now say,

"WHAT JUSTICE
DEMANDS."

All eyes are on Moses. He looks across the faces in the multitude with respect, humility, and gentleness. His stance is relaxed, yet his feet are planted with boldness. He says:

> "Kings and queens of the Most High, I have a new insight about justice.
>
> "Our experience together has filled in the meaning of Adam's question to us. Adam asked us, 'Do souls serve justice, or

does justice serve souls?' The answer to Adam's question is that justice serves souls. I can now explain to you an insight into *how* justice serves souls."

Moses turns to the Lord, bows low, and says, "Righteousness and justice are the foundation of your throne forever."

Moses gestures toward the scroll that is tucked within Adam's belt. (This is the scroll Adam had pulled from Moses' beard.) Adam nods and passes it to Moses.

Moses begins to scan the scroll's contents. Moses points down at the scroll and then lifts his finger into the air. Golden words appear. Moses reads the words, saying:

"Give justice to the weak and
the fatherless; maintain the
right of the afflicted and the
destitute."

Moses then rolls up the scroll and holds it in his right hand. He lifts the scroll into the air and addresses the multitude:

"In this scroll of the Lord's revelation, you can see that the purpose of the Lord's justice is to *make things right*. His justice makes things right for the weak, the fatherless, the destitute, the victims of theft and manipulation, and for all those who have been harmed in any way. When things are made right, there is justice. When things are not made right, there is no justice.

"There is a mystery in the Lord's justice. On the surface of justice, you see that people should get what they deserve. But what do people deserve?

"Some people, in their zeal to carry out justice, have instead carried out revenge. Revenge is justice turned upside down. Revenge multiplies wrongs, while the Lord's justice makes things right.

"In light of this understanding of the Lord's justice, I offer a question for your consideration: *how* can wrongs be made right? What methods bring true justice into the world?"

Moses pauses to give room for thought. He then says:

"To make things right, what was destroyed must be made whole. What was injured must be healed. What was broken must be restored. I tell you, therefore, that justice is not fully established until *everything* is fully made right, including every broken relationship."

Moses turns to Eve. He says:

"Eve, I know your children have endured many injustices. In order for justice to be fulfilled, things need to be made right again. Those who became weak need to be made strong. Those who had no father need to have a father. Justice demands that what was stolen from you and your children must be restored."

Eve nods her head in agreement. Moses turns back to the multitude. He continues:

"There was something stolen from all of us that only Lucifer could restore to us. We lost the potential to experience his unique glory and gifts. Our relationship to him was broken. Our joy of knowing Lucifer in his pure goodness was lost. Lucifer's unique and special love could not reach us. Nor could his songs. A special relationship with this being was stolen from us.

"Hear me, my friends: all the riches of heaven are insufficient to make up for a lost relationship. As long as someone is separated from us, our heavenly celebration cannot be complete."

Moses turns to Adam. Moses says:

"You were right, Adam. Justice serves souls. Indeed, justice has demands that are vastly greater than I had previously imagined. Justice demands that things be made right. So, meeting *all* the demands of justice requires making *all* things right."

Adam lifts his eyebrows. He seems a bit surprised to hear Moses expressing these ideas about justice. You can tell that Adam is pondering Moses' words, and that the thought of them delights him.

Moses turns to Lucifer. He says:

"As the Lord has said, the chamber of torment was necessary for your restoration. Your restoration was necessary to make right our relationship with you. Today things have been made right *in* you and *with* you. The purpose of the Lord's justice has been fulfilled."

The golden words above the door form into another key. The key descends into Moses' hands. Moses says,

"This key is the third insight: *justice is fulfilled when things are made right.*"

Moses inserts the key into the glowing lock on the door. He steps back and says, "Open." The lock opens. The chain falls to the ground. Four locks remain.

Moses steps back, and the Lord gestures toward Adam. "Adam, you have new revelation," the Lord says with a gentle smile.

Adam says, "Yes. I see something I didn't see before. I have come to understand the agreements that we made before we were born."

"Come, Adam," the Lord invites. "Share with us what you see."

Adam steps forward toward the door. The fourth lock and chain radiate with a brilliant light. Adam touches the lock, and the golden letters above the door change form. They say,

"ANCIENT AGREEMENTS."

Adam is now facing the multitude. Adam says,

"Listen, my friends. I have seen a great truth. Do you know that everything serves souls? Just as justice serve souls, I have learned that the ancient agreements also serve souls.

"We heard from Moses that before we were born, we agreed to embark on a hero's journey. I now understand this agreement. I now see its wisdom. This wisdom appeared in my heart when I saw Lucifer break free from his torment.

"Let me tell you: at first, I was completely puzzled by the agreements. When Moses told us about them, I didn't understand why the Lord would sanction an agreement that could result in infinite loss. We heard this agreement was as strong as the Lord's throne; it could not be broken. I was perplexed by how an agreement could be so strong.

"But then, when I saw Lucifer break free, I realized that souls do not serve agreements. The reverse is true. *Agreements serve souls.*

"Listen, my friends: no contract has authority on its own. All authority comes from those who make the contract. Do you see? If those who make a contract all agree to cancel it, then that contract is cancelled.

"If we did indeed make an agreement before we were born, we could agree to cancel that agreement. By the law of grace, we can cancel any agreement we agree to cancel.

"It all is very obvious now. As surely as the Lord's throne serves the Lord, agreements serve souls. If the Lord's throne stops serving the Lord, the Lord may destroy it. And, if an agreement between souls stops serving them, those souls may agree to destroy that agreement. If, together, we all agree to make it so, it shall be so.

"Agreements are the source of all creation! They precede every law and every action. When planets orbit a star, their orbit follows a law of motion. The laws of motion are agreements between the Lord and Himself. Every law is an agreement, and every action proceeds from an agreement.

"I say it again: agreements are under the authority of royal beings. That is why we could liberate Lucifer. We agreed to liberate him. The authority was in our hands to free the dark soul from the debt he owed us."

The golden words form into a key. The key drifts down, and Adam grabs the key with one hand. Adam says,

"This key is the fourth insight: *ancient agreements are the basis of order, but even ancient agreements can be broken if they no longer serve souls.*"

Adam puts the key into the next lock on the door. Adam says, "Open." The lock opens. The chain falls to the ground. Three locks remain.

Adam steps back, and the Lord says to Eve, "Eve, what do you see?" The Lord brushes His hand to one side, inviting Eve to stand beside Him.

Eve approaches the golden door. Once she has reached the Lord's side, the fifth lock and chain begin to glow. The golden letters above the door transform. They say,

"YOUR HIDDEN GLORY."

Eve takes a couple steps forward. She looks down as she gathers her thoughts, and then she lovingly looks upon the sea of faces gazing back at her. She speaks in a gentle, yet powerful, voice:

"My dear sons and daughters, I see something now that I have never fully understood. We heard that the Lord hid Lucifer's glory so that his glory would be discovered and displayed in time. My glory was also hidden. Like Lucifer, I had a desire for my glory to be displayed. But I came to believe this desire was entirely selfish and needed to be suppressed. Many of my children—many of *you*—also believed that God did not desire for your glory be revealed. I didn't understand that the Lord wanted my glory to be sought after so that it could be displayed. He wanted me to be on display, as His beautiful creature.

"Listen, my children: it was never forbidden for me to be like God. I desired something I *already had*. I was already created in the likeness of God. We all are.

"Although I did not retaliate against the Lord, I assumed I could never have everything my heart desired. I felt something had to be held back. And, indeed, many times my desires were frustrated. So, I buried my desires under layers of hidden emotions. I underestimated the generosity and wisdom of our Lord.

"Many souls are separated from the Lord because they don't understand the fullness of the Lord's love for them. They don't know that the Lord wants them to have the deepest desires of their heart.

"Do you desire attention and affection? The Lord desires that you receive attention and affection. Do you desire to be on display? The Lord desires to put all His creatures on display. He hides only the greatest treasures, so that they may be sought and discovered.

"As Lucifer spoke about God's desire to hide great things, I understood what he meant. The Lord hides great things for kings to search out and discover. There are glories in every place and within every being that still await discovery.

"My fellow kings and queens, you are designed to rule and reign with the Lord. You desire to be great because you are great! You are all greater than you can ever fully comprehend. We all are. We are so great because our Lord is so great, and we are made in His likeness."

The words above the golden door transform into a key and gently land in Eve's hands. Eve says,

> "This key is the fifth insight: *your desire to be great comes from your inner glory, which reflects the glory of the Greatest Being.*"

Eve takes the key into one hand and inserts the key into the glowing lock. "Open," she says as she takes a step back. The lock opens. The chain falls to the ground. Two locks remain.

Eve steps back, and the Lord says to Lucifer, "Lucifer, tell us what you see."

The Lord invites Lucifer to stand beside Him. Lucifer gracefully glides to the Lord's side and touches the next lock, which has begun to glow brightly.

The golden letters above the golden door display the words,

> *"YOUR GREATEST PURPOSE."*

Lucifer's stance is timid and humble. He looks back at the Lord, who puts his hand on Lucifer's shoulder. This strengthens Lucifer and gives him courage to speak. Lucifer turns to behold the humans. He says,

"You, beloved humans, were born in a lowly condition. Your lives began in darkness. I was born in a high condition. I began in light. Your lowly condition was part of a kingdom that looked upside down to me. I now see that my kingdom was upside down. I understand that those who are low shall be raised up, and those who are high shall be made low. All these things are part of a great purpose to reveal glories of goodness in all creation and in our Creator.

"After you released me from my torment, the Lord revealed to me who I am. At the center of His revelation was a knowledge of my true value. The Lord said to me, 'You are glorious. I made you with an everlasting glory that only you have, and only you can have. Every creature has unique glory. So too, there is no glory like your glory. I want everyone to see your glory. In your glory, you are made to rule and reign.'"

Lucifer motions to Moses, and Moses hands Lucifer the scroll Moses is holding. Lucifer opens the scroll and then points.

He says, "It is written, 'I was once lost but now am found.'"

Lucifer moves to another section of the scroll and then says, "It is also written, 'the beast will come out of the deep and go to its destruction.' Did you know, Moses, that the words 'destruction' and 'lost' are translations of the *same root word?*"

Moses shakes his head, "I hadn't noticed that."

Lucifer continues, "Yes, the root meaning is the same. Listen, Moses. I was very lost. But now I am found. I was completely destroyed. But now I am completely restored."

Lucifer points again to the scroll, and says,

> "Moses, there are many hints of hope in the scrolls. Look here. It is written, 'every knee will bow before me; every tongue will acknowledge God.'
>
> "Some have said that the Lord will get everyone to bow before Him, whether they want to or not. Inside this frame of understanding, some souls will only acknowledge God out of fear and hatred.

"But I ask you, what does it mean to *truly acknowledge* God?

"I stand before you to acknowledge and declare the glory of God. I tell you, the Lord does not rule with control and fear, as I did. He does not *make* people acknowledge Him. His kingdom flips the kingdom of darkness upside down. The Lord rules with love, which casts out fear. The Lord never arranges for anyone to bow before Him *in fear*. Instead, He never stops working to bring all His enemies under His feet *in love*. "

Lucifer turns his attention back to the crowd. He continues:

"Good and evil are not symmetric. The good is infinitely greater than the evil. From every evil, there is potential for good to spring. In the *greatest* evil, there is potential for the *greatest* good.

"I reveal to you a great truth. Listen. If *I* can be turned around, every evil can be turned around. There is always hope. Your fundamental purpose is to transform evil by the power of your love."

The golden words above the door form into a key. Lucifer says,

> "This key is the sixth insight: *your love has the power to transform any evil.*"

The key floats into Lucifer's hand. He steps forward and places the key into the lock. Lucifer says, "Open." The lock opens. The chain falls to the ground. One lock remains.

Lucifer steps back as the final lock and chain begin to glow.

"Who has the final insight to open the final lock?" you wonder.

The Lord steps forward and looks toward the door. He then looks down toward the ground. He stoops down and begins to write something on the ground with His finger.

Everyone is curious. What is the Lord doing?

After a few moments, the Lord peels up from the ground what looks like a large piece of parchment. As He peels it up, it rolls up like a scroll.

The Lord turns to Moses and offers the scroll to him. "I know you love scrolls, Moses," the glorious man says with a smile.

Moses accepts the scroll and holds it before him with both hands. "But Lord," Moses inquires, "what is this scroll?"

The Lord begins to chuckle. "You will soon find out," the Lord laughs as He reaches out and touches the final lock on the golden door. The shining letters above the golden door say,

"THE MEANING OF IT ALL."

The Lord steps back from the door and gestures for Moses to stand beside Him. Moses draws close. The Lord asks Moses, "Will you read for us what is written on the scroll?"

Moses nods and unrolls the scroll. He looks down at the scroll. A smile spreads across his face. He looks up toward the multitude and speaks:

"Kings and queens of the Inner Courts, I present to you a message from the Lord. This message illuminates a great meaning in everything we have seen today. Hear what the Lord says..."

Moses clears his throat. He lowers his voice and loudly reads:

"He who is forgiven much loves much."

Moses' voice echoes across the multitude, and then it fades away into silence. Soon afterward, you hear something very quiet. It is a muffled chuckle. You scan the faces and see that the laughter is coming from Lucifer. There are tears in his eyes as he laughs. You can tell he is trying to hold his laughter in. But his efforts are of no use. Soon, Lucifer's laughter is uncontainable. The Lord joins the angel in his laughter.

The laughter spreads to everyone gathered around the Lord's throne. The laughter is as rich and thick as honey, but as mighty as thunder. This is the loudest and most powerful laugher anyone has ever felt.

Laughter continues for what feels like ages and ages. Then, the laughing turns into a song of worship. All the creatures of heaven join in the magnificent display of worship to the Lord.

Within the multitude gathers a group of the most brilliant and skilled artists, singers, musicians, dancers, and actors. The group includes people of Earth as well as a host of angels.

Adam says to Lucifer, "Our worship is mature, but your worship is pure and deep. Your worship goes deeper than ours ever could. Please, lead us."

Lucifer looks toward the host of beings that have begun gathering around him. There is a twinkle in his eye. Something within him has awakened with purpose. It is a part of him that has been dormant for an eternity past. But it has never left him.

Lucifer begins giving instructions to those who have gathered around him. Those with instruments begin to learn their parts. Singers bring new lyrics of worship into their hearts. Some are skilled with mixing flavors and scents, and they prepare oil, incense, and perfume. Actors prepare to dramatize a story that touches the deepest emotions of the soul. Artists sculpt and paint and sketch beautiful imagery. This imagery leads minds and hearts on a journey of closer encounters with the love of the Living Source of All.

Lucifer leads all of heaven into the sweetest, richest, deepest experience of worship the beings of heaven have ever known.

As the worship continues, the golden words above the golden door form into a key. The Lord reaches up and takes the key into His hand. The Lord says,

"This key is the seventh insight: *the greatest evil can turn into the greatest love.*"

He inserts the key into the final lock. The Lord says, "Open." The lock opens. The final chain falls to the ground.

The golden door now stands free and clear, unlocked and ready to open.

CHAPTER ELEVEN

The Golden Door Opens

T HE LORD, in brilliant human form, stands before the golden door. There is a smile on the Lord's face. With eyes of love, He speaks to everyone gathered:

"Dear Friends," the Lord says, "the golden door is now ready to open. Seven secrets bound this door for ages and ages. Those secrets have been unlocked. You now carry within you a wisdom that grants you the power to open the door and step through."

The Lord senses a question resounding through the hearts and minds of the multitude. Everyone wants to know:

*"What awaits us on the other
side of this golden door?"*

The Lord raises His arms in a welcoming embrace. The Lord proclaims:

"I will now explain to you what this golden door is, how it came to be, and what will happen if it is opened."

All are quiet. Everyone listens attentively as the Lord tells the story of the golden door.

"A long time ago, the Eternal Source, which is my essence, enjoyed harmony with all created beings. The Eternal Source created many realms for many beings. In every realm, joy, love, and goodness sprang forth in many flavors and colors.

"As creatures explored the universe, some creatures formed a desire for greater separation from their Source. They began to depart from the purest forms of light. As they moved further away from their Source, they began to experience twisted forms of wisdom and pleasure. Corruption entered their lives. They became dark souls.

"The Eternal Source sustained them with love. Nevertheless, the dark souls continued to forge paths away from the light. They pushed further and further away from the fountain of goodness and wisdom.

"One day, the evil beings approached the Eternal Source and said, 'Ancient One, we feel that your power is too great and your rule too broad. Your presence is overbearing. We desire to rule apart from you. We desire a kingdom of our own.

"'Prepare for us a place where you will not enter—where you will not interfere. Promise us you will not come into our presence, lest you overwhelm us with grief.

"'We desire freedom. We want independence from you so that we may create a kingdom in whatever way we desire. Make an agreement with us this day, so that our joy may be complete.'

"The Eternal Source replied, 'What you desire, you shall have. I have prepared a place for you to exist independent of my light and rule. From now on, I agree to let you reign far away from me.

"'I will not come into your kingdom with glory or power. If I seek an audience with the king of your realm, I will assume no authority that he does not grant me.

"'As a sign of our agreement, I have created this golden door. I will seal this door with seven locks. This door is a symbol of the chasm between our kingdoms. No one may pass from my kingdom to yours, or from your kingdom to mine.'

"The dark souls replied in delight, 'Yes, this agreement seems right to us. We will allow you to enter, but only to speak with our king. When you enter our kingdom, you must leave your power behind.

"'Our king will do the same. He may enter your place to speak with you, but he must leave his power behind. Yes, this plan seems right to us, for then our kingdoms will not be easy to mix.'

"The Eternal Source replied, 'Very well. Only the kings may cross from one kingdom to the other. Everyone else will be held back.'

"'But,' the dark souls asked hesitantly, 'what if, one day, those who are in your kingdom desire to depart from there and join us? Can we increase our kingdom with new souls?'

"The Eternal Source replied, 'As I create new worlds, I will allow you an opportunity to spread the reaches of your kingdom onto those worlds. Souls who enter one of these worlds may enter your kingdom by the appointed doorways. Any soul who wants to join your kingdom may come under your rule. Any soul who wants to join my kingdom will come under my rule, and they will be protected by the golden door.'

"The dark souls asked, 'What if those who come under your rule want to leave your kingdom and come into ours? Will you unlock the golden door for them?'

"The Eternal Source answered, 'I will provide a way to open the door for any citizen of my kingdom who wants to come into your kingdom. To unlock the golden door will require understanding.'

"'We have one more question,' the dark souls replied. 'What if someone from your kingdom unlocks the golden door? Can we still stop them from coming through the golden door if we wish?'

"The Eternal Source answered, 'No one may come into your kingdom through the golden door without the permission of your king.'

"'Yes, this agreement seems right to us,' the dark souls said. 'Those who learn to open the door may enter through it if our king allows. Yes, it is right.'

"'Do you agree to these terms?' the Eternal Source asked them.

"'Yes, may it be done as you have said,' the dark souls squealed with excitement.

"Thus, the Eternal Source sealed the agreement. Those who wanted to be separated from the Eternal Source formed their own kingdom. No citizen of heaven would have the power to enter their kingdom without going through the golden door. And no one could pass through the golden door, unless the king of the dark souls agreed.

"The realm that lies beyond the golden door is the kingdom of hell. This is the place I prepared for the Dark One and all of his subjects. And its king is now standing in your midst—Lucifer, the glorious angel, who has returned to the Eternal Source."

A hush falls over the multitude. Adam steps forward and says, "You had even greater purposes than we dreamed. You brought the king of darkness here, to this place, to change his heart. You did this so that he would grant us permission to enter through the golden door." Adam's expression is enlightened, and his tone is thoughtful. You can feel that the statement he is expressing is profound.

"Yes, Adam," the Lord replies. "It was the only way to open a pathway to restore all souls to light and life."

The Lord turns to Lucifer. He asks, "Do these souls standing here have your permission to enter through the golden door?"

Lucifer bows low to the ground. He looks up at the Lord and says, "If the citizens of your kingdom can bring life to the separated souls, let us delay no longer! I grant all those here permission to enter through the golden door!"

The Lord grasps the jewel-studded handle of the golden door. He pulls the door. The door opens very slowly.

Once the door is open just a crack, dark smoke creeps upward from it in thin ribbons. As the door opens wider, the smoke thickens and billows upward into a long, black plume.

The smoke clears a bit, and you can see only darkness beyond. You hear the voices of countless souls suffering, cursing, weeping, and screaming. The place beyond the golden door is a dreadful place.

The Lord holds up His hands and gestures for everyone to pay attention.

> "Citizens of my kingdom, I will now give you your assignments and tell you what to expect next."

The Lord looks with compassion upon His people. He says to them:

> "There are souls beyond this golden door who are ready to see new light. Some will be more resistant than others.
>
> "Your assignment is to bring jewels of wisdom and virtue to these suffering souls so that their suffering may come to an end. Bring them the good news that there is a way out of the darkness. Help them recognize the love that is already given to them. Help them to forgive, as they have been forgiven. Help them to heal the relationships that have been broken.

"Some of the souls have already resisted attempts to free them. You might recognize some of these souls as tyrants of old. Do not fear, my children. You have gained much authority and insight from your experience; you have more power, virtue, and wisdom than you had before.

"The assignment I offer you is not easy. I will provide you with shields of protection, but I cannot guarantee that your hearts will not ache. This assignment is risky, but the reward is great.

"As you enter the realm of hell beyond, you will discover that the task of rescuing souls is not as simple as pulling them from the fire. The hell they are experiencing outwardly is also embedded in them internally. In these souls, there is a kingdom of darkness.

"I told the people of Earth ages ago, 'the kingdom of heaven is within you.' Those whose hearts are whole, who display virtue, who live in both generosity and abundance, have heaven inside of them. You have seen the glorious riches, abundance, beauty, and virtue of the place in which you now dwell. But I tell you, whoever cultivates heaven within themselves will bring the reality of heaven into the world outside themselves.

"Likewise, as you help the inhabitants of hell to bring heaven into their hearts, the very nature of hell can be transformed. The highest mission before us, then, is not merely to rescue souls from hell. The highest mission is to transform hell into heaven.

"May you embark on this assignment out of the abundance of love in your hearts. May you make love grow in new places.

"You may decide how to proceed. Some of you may decide to venture into this treacherous realm on your own. You may decide to gather together with others to develop a strategy. You may decide to use the method of teaching, or you may decide to bring revelation in other creative forms. The mission is to restore the separated souls to wholeness and life so that they may enter into their full greatness and be united with us in love."

The Lord looks across the multitude and asks:

"Who will accept this mission?"

All across the multitude, you see people raising their hands and pressing forward in eagerness.

The Lord steps back from the door and waves His arms toward it. "Enter, brave ones. Your reward is great in heaven."

You hear snippets of conversations of people who have begun moving toward the golden door. People are developing strategies. Some have gathered together instruments and works of art. Others have prepared testimonies and stories. The Lord puts upon His people a suit of golden armor as they approach the door. Once they have been equipped, the Lord sends them through the door. Countless souls file through the door, eager to embark on the mission.

A thought occurs to you: *"This is the day when heaven invades hell."*

Filled with excitement, you begin to follow the others as they move toward the door. You watch in anticipation as those before you receive their armor and enter through the golden doorway.

You are next in line. You step forward so that you are face to face with the Lord. The Lord looks gently into your eyes and puts His hand on your shoulder.

The Lord says, "My precious child, you are not ready."

You ask, "Why not?" You are sincerely surprised by the Lord's response.

The Lord replies, "Your soul is young. Your experiences are few. The place these souls are going takes robust, radical love. It takes heroic love. It takes a love filled out by the meaning of many experiences. All those who invade hell must first embark on a hero's journey. Before you join these others, you must first be born into a world where you can experience your own hero's journey."

You are curious to know more. You have little knowledge or experience to inform you of what the true meaning of a hero's journey actually is. Your eyes look deep into the Lord's eyes.

The Lord draws closer to you. He whispers into your ear, "Are you ready for an adventure?"

You feel something leap inside you. Desire gives birth to a response: "Yes, Lord, send me on a hero's journey."

"Yes, my child, I will send you," says the Lord. The Lord cups His hands, and a small translucent image appears there, between you and the Lord. "I was thinking of sending you here. I believe you are well-fitted to bring my love into this place. I also think you will enjoy many aspects of the life you can create here."

You inspect the image. You feel the emotions, the adventure, the risk, the challenges, and the great potential represented by the image before you. The adventure this image represents excites you. "Yes, Lord. I will go here."

Tears form in the Lord's eyes as He offers you these parting words:

> "I love you so much. My love for you will never fade. It will never end. May you always remember my love for you.
>
> "What lies ahead will be difficult. There will be darkness. There will be pain. There will be uncertainty.
>
> "But in the darkness, greatness develops. Insights emerge. Virtues spring. My voice will always be with you.
>
> "May you never forget the glory I have put inside you. May you never forget my love.
>
> "Bring my love to the other souls who have forgotten. Never stop seeking for the good gifts I have hidden for you to discover. Never stop seeking to discover the fullness of who I created you to be. Remember my love. Remember."

As the Lord speaks, everything around you disappears. All grows dark. You are surrounded in complete warmth and peace. As you rest in the darkness, your memories begin to fade.

You rest in complete peace for what seems like ages. In a moment, your experience changes. You feel pressure. There is pain. A bright light blinds you. You gasp for breath and begin to cry.

You sense other souls around you. You cannot tell who they are. They seem foreign to you. Yet, you are comforted by their voices and their touch.

Peace is within you, yet you begin to experience needs and desires. You cannot comprehend where you are or who you are. You are completely vulnerable.

What lies ahead is uncertain. Yet, you have a great purpose from the Lord, who is the Source of light and life. You have been given unique gifts to explore and to use to love others.

There will be challenges, but you will never quit. You understand, deep inside, that your purpose is great. You are great.

Your assignment is embedded in your DNA. You will shine your unique light into dark places. You will invade places where hell holds its grip. You will love courageously. You will heal the brokenhearted. You will bring a taste of heaven into this world.

As you go about your mission, you are training for the greatest adventure in history. You are a hero in the greatest story ever told.

EPILOGUE

WHILE THIS BOOK is a work of fiction, not every part of this book departs from reality.

We have written this book from the conviction that every person has measureless worth and unending purposes. We hope this book has encouraged you.

We recognize that there is not currently a consensus among the people of Earth concerning the destiny of souls. Can those who are lost at death be made alive again? While we make no claim about actual events, we want to leave you with hope of a greater vision of reality. We believe that the principles of justice, love, and purpose described in this book transcend every possible world. These principles point to your great value and to your purposes on Earth.

We believe that your unique journey is very important. You have a role to play in the Great Story, the story of all souls. You have a great power to transform the world around you with a special touch and style. You have a unique flavor of heaven inside of you. It is good that you are in this world.

So, what work will you choose to pursue in your own hero's journey?

May the heaven within you invade the places of hell around you. May you bring more of heaven into the earth. And may the quiet voice of the guiding light within you draw you into greater and greater realms of glory.

May the Eternal One be with you always!

Many blessings,
Rachel and Joshua Rasmussen

P.S. Thank you for reading!

We realize this book may have raised many thoughts or questions for you, and we don't want to leave you hanging!

We have created a website to facilitate discussion for our readers, as well as to share valuable resources with you, including references to materials you may find helpful if you desire to study any of the topics in this book in more depth.

To access additional resources and supplemental materials, to participate in community discussions, or to contact us with your thoughts, questions, or feedback, please visit our website at *invadinghell.com.*

Printed in Great Britain
by Amazon